TAGE TALĒS

the falling woman

Vintage Tales

the

falling

STORIES

SHAENA LAMBERT

woman

VINTAGE CANADA

VINTAGE CANADA EDITION, 2002

National Library of Canada Cataloguing in Publication Data

Lambert, Shaena

The falling woman

ISBN 0-679-31149-1

I. Title.

PS8573.A3985F34 2002   C813'.6   C2001-903483-0

PR9199.4.L34F34 2002

Text design: CS Richardson

Printed and bound in Canada

This book is printed on 100% recycled, 100% post-consumer waste paper.

www.randomhouse.ca

2 4 6 8 9 7 5 3 1

For Bob and for Wendy

contents

Vintage Tales

resistance

THE DAY OF DANIEL'S CONFESSION started in an ordinary way, with a call from Kaye's mother—a beginning that Kaye would examine in detail later (poking at it, parsing it), trying to find clues to what she had known and what she hadn't. In the morning she hadn't known what was going to happen, but by the time she went to bed she knew everything. In between she found out that her husband was sleeping with a girl of twenty-six, a master's student of his from the environmental studies department, a girl who might have been a younger, shabbier, messier version of Kaye herself. Or at least one part of herself—the lean, uncompromising self she had been at one time.

But the day had begun as those days usually did, with the scramble to pack a lunch for Sarah, the hasty goodbyes at the door, the moment of silence—then the call from Kaye's mother.

"Kaye!" Margaret exclaimed lavishly, making Kaye wince.

"Mother!" Kaye exclaimed back. "Why do you always sound surprised when it's me? You're the one phoning."

Kaye's mother threw back her head and laughed

richly. What a lark her daughter was. What a perfect straight man. Kaye knew her mother had thrown back her head and laughed even though she couldn't see her, she was *that* present in the room. Like a very large ghost, she filled the area above Kaye's head with her dyed ash-blond hair, her burgundy nails, her legs stubbled with persistent growth. She had yards and yards of female *pulchritude*. A hideous word, yes, but one that Kaye had chosen long ago to describe her mother's particular kind of beauty.

"Now listen, honey, have you got a minute? Has Daniel left? Has Sarah left for school?"

They had left, it was true. And it was also true that no matter how irritated Kaye sometimes felt at the sound of her mother's voice, she liked these calls, she waited for these calls.

They were close, mother and daughter. They had stuck together through thick and thin. Thick mother, thin daughter, Kaye thought—because sometimes it felt like that; as though her mother, that plentiful and immense woman, cast such a shadow, and contained so much, that she contained even Kaye herself.

People noticed their closeness. They compared Margaret with their own mothers, in their late fifties or early sixties, and said that Kaye was lucky, because her mother was so interesting, so alive. Other mothers had receded, becoming pale, or frosty, or diffident; or taking up causes. Daniel's mother had become a pro-choice activist in Sudbury, defying the church, defying her husband. Interesting, of course—but nothing to match the livid, arresting quality that Margaret gave off.

At fifty-nine she was in her prime, magnificently in her prime, like a full-blown moon—carrying all her past selves inside. Retired actress. Radio host. Now she and Kaye's father had bought a sailboat, and they headed up the coast each summer scouting for northwest coast sculptures, bartering, collecting. She had become known for her talent, her eye. Someone famous in Ketchikan had even given her a Tlingit name.

Now Margaret was telling Kaye a story about Kaye's father. He had become a source of bafflement and amusement to them since he had retired. They watched him as though he were a peculiar and interesting bird—something, perhaps, with a rare, proboscis-like beak. Last month he had started reading Proust—five pages a night. "He always hated Proust!" Margaret said to Kaye. "His mother made him read Proust to her in that ugly room she never left, with aspidistra hanging from the bedstead. I can't believe he's reading Proust." But this was nothing compared with what he had done the day before on their yacht. It had been a suddenly warm day for October, an Indian summer day, and Margaret, in a mood of celebration, had peeled off her shirt, slathered her breasts with baby oil and stretched out on the foredeck. Giles had slipped away from the wheel to get his sunglasses, forgotten why he'd gone below deck and settled in for a little nap.

"Kaye—picture it—all at once we're careening towards an enormous freighter from Taiwan. I had to crawl across the deck, throw something over me, grab the wheel. Meanwhile, about fifteen deckhands had caught sight of me, and they were all cheering madly."

As was so often the case, once her mother got going, Kaye felt something dark stirring inside her: a feeling that her mother had escaped scot-free, gotten away with the gold or some such thing, while she—Kaye—was caught. Punished.

"Listen," Margaret continued. "I read something in the *Sun* this morning and I thought you'd get a kick out of it. Apparently there's this real estate agent in Topeka, Kansas—and guess what he's doing."

"Mother, I couldn't possibly."

"He's buying up abandoned missile silos all over the Midwest and he's turning them into houses. Can you imagine! And apparently people are buying them like hotcakes."

"Perfect for the nuclear family."

"Oh, honey—when I read that, I couldn't help thinking of you, back in your anti-nuclear days. You could be so ornery."

"Not precisely how I remember it, Mother."

"Oh, come on. You were damned ornery, you have to admit it. Do you remember that time you destroyed our dinner party?"

Kaye's heart was beating slightly faster. Of course she remembered. It was a frequent memory, a talisman, something she carried with her even now, almost twenty years later.

It was back when her parents lived in Shaughnessy and she was in first-year university. She had plunked herself down on the burgundy couch in the living room and one of her mother's friends had asked her, just casually, what she was doing to keep herself busy. Kaye had answered that she and some other students were organizing a viewing of *If You Love This Planet*.

"Oh, Helen Caldicott," Lena Marsden had shrieked. "She's ghastly."

"A ghoul, darling. She's a ghoul!"

"She'd be more bearable if she got her facts straight." This was from one of the straight men—an accountant, like her father. One of the dull spouses.

It was then that Kaye had risen into the air—or so it had felt—springing out of her seat to float above them, an angel of vengeance and light. Then she had described, point by point, what the effect would be of a nuclear bomb dropped on Vancouver. Yes, she had done this a bit breathlessly; yes, with a red face and palpitating heart; but nevertheless she had recited the whole thing—the sacred litany of destruction—from the fallout floating up as far as the troposphere, to the lack of burn beds, the disease, the lacerations, decapitations, wind fires. "And if you did survive in a fallout shelter," she had said, "when you came out, there would be rotting corpses everywhere—because ninety percent of Vancouver's population would be dead—and the survivors would soon die too, from a synergistic combination of starvation, radiation, sunburn, infection and grief."

At which point—at least in Kaye's recollection—her mother had stood up and said, in her rich actor's voice, that she did hope everyone was ready for dinner.

"You were the absolute death of dinner parties," Kaye's mother said now, always thrilled by a spectacle, even in retrospect.

And what could Kaye possibly say in response? She looked out the window at the clear sky and a plane high up, like a toy, heading towards the airport.

She wanted to say that perhaps her mother should rethink her attitude. Had the prospect of nuclear war really been all *that* funny? In the old days that's what she would have said, and for a second she wished that she could still be that single-minded. The insistence of the young. *We are born once,* they had sung. *Born for a purpose.* And they had circled the weapons, singing and crying, throwing their bodies again and again against this huge dark wall, this impenetrable thing.

But that was over now. She wasn't that person any more. And people were living in the silos that she had prayed in front of. Turning them into condos.

Kaye was a librarian. And there was no question that she looked like one, with her brown hair clipped in a neat bob, her tasselled leather shoes and neutral sweater sets. She was a small, hipless woman, five feet tall in her stockinged feet, who amazed her friends by buying her pyjamas and T-shirts in the boys' department of the Bay. But, despite her conventional appearance, Kaye did have streaks in her character that indicated a varied past life. The largest of these, of course, was the fact of her criminal background, her numerous arrests, chalked up in Toronto while doing her post-graduate degree in librarianship.

Sometimes Gayla, another librarian at the Vancouver Public Library, encouraged Kaye to elaborate.

How many times were you arrested, Kaye? Come on. Tell us.

Gayla was proud of Kaye. Proud of her smallness and neatness, which could wondrously unfold and expand, a bit like a sponge animal, to reveal her peculiar past.

How many times were you arrested?

Eleven.

Longest arrest?

Three weeks.

And why were you arrested, Kaye?

Seven times for repeatedly chaining herself to a fence at Litton. Once for throwing paint on a car that contained the minister of national defence. Twice for obstructing the flow of traffic through downtown Toronto (she had chained herself to a block of cement in the middle of Yonge Street, to stop a plutonium shipment). And once— this was for three weeks—for climbing over a high-security fence in North Dakota to sit on top of a buried missile silo. She had been lucky that time, she was told; that kind of crime could have meant years in jail.

And how did you meet Daniel? Come on. Tell us.

Sitting in the library cafeteria, Kaye would cross her ankles, tuck a bit of stray hair behind her ear and say yes, it was true, she had met her now university-professor husband in jail.

It was after one of the mass demonstrations at Litton. The RCMP had thrown Kaye into a windowless room divided by bars into two small cells. They knew she was one of the leaders; knew because they had seen her at other demonstrations. And because she was an expert at being arrested—going limp, continuing to sing even as they carried her away, yelling that nothing could stop them from laying themselves down, resisting death with their bodies.

After a while the guards had thrown Daniel into the cell next to hers. She had seen him at rallies but had never spoken to him before. He was big and bear-like, with deep brown eyes, and he was wearing a poncho and Birkenstocks, so that he looked quite a bit like a desert prophet. And such a hairy man! He had bristles on his chin, hair on his knuckles, even some noticeable bits of hair sticking out from the nostrils of his large nose. Seeing this made Kaye think of something she had read once, about how old people's noses and ears keep growing and growing as they age, even though the rest of their bodies stop growing or even shrink. This would definitely happen to Daniel. It was only a matter of time and then his nose would become immense, and dark hairs would jut from it, fascinating and intimidating his grandchildren.

In the middle of the night, he told her about where he had grown up, near Sudbury. It was a place he evoked easily, full of Jack pine forests and unintentional malice, where on dates they drove out to the pit mine to watch the hot nickel being poured down a concrete flume. It was a place where rape, like bad water, seemed to be a constant that went with the poverty. As he talked, Kaye had the impression all at once that perhaps people weren't supposed to get over their bad childhoods. Maybe, instead, all those memories were supposed to become like this— tangled thickets that existed all the time, just underneath, places that held their own kind of attraction. Just the way he said *Sudbury* made the whole place open up: the dirt tracks through the woods, the spray of molten metal, the death of his sister caused by the meaningless conjunction of a yellow tractor and a drunken uncle.

After talking to her mother, Kaye went and stood at the back door and looked out at the yard. It was a cool, clear day, the sudden warm spell over. Not rainy, either, although the weather report had predicted rain. The sky was blue, with wisps of cloud in it, and the grass was beaten down, gleaming from the first frost. The metal clothes tree in the yard, a remnant from another era, shone like something beautiful and alien. Through the hedge of cedars she glimpsed the back lane, a bit of the neighbour's white garage, then two huge golden maples, their leaves a shock of colour against the sky.

She felt a small shiver of irritation, like ants walking over her back, at the thought of her mother laughing over her father reading Proust. They probably read it to each other on the sailboat. She opened the door and breathed in deeply. The air smelled of frost and decomposing leaves. A clean smell.

Somehow her parents had escaped. They hadn't even looked back for her, they'd just gone—reading Proust to each other, having fabulous sex in their sailboat, making their way up the Inside Passage, mooring in secret coves. They would make the simple meals they both loved, frying juicy steaks, eating them with boiled potatoes, talking about what they had seen that day. Her mother would speculate about the family they had moored beside that morning at a government wharf, making up a small story about them—affairs, trivialities, a mistress left behind—and Kaye's father would laugh amiably. A thin man now, with withered skin on his arms, age spots on his bird-like face. A man with white hair, white summer loafers, pale blue Ralph Lauren shirts. He would hold out his plate for more potatoes, and she would cut one in half, serve him.

And so what? Kaye thought. Wasn't that allowed? She breathed in deeply again. One of her neighbours was burning leaves, ignoring the ordinances. She could hear children's voices coming from the Catholic school a block away, children released for recess.

Her parents had come a long way—that was all—come a long way from the days when they would fight and scream and pitch things at each other, like Ralph and Alice from *The Honeymooners*, or Punch and Judy. Bouncing ironing boards on each other's heads, winging butter dishes at the wall. One time he had locked Margaret out of the house in her underwear and she had smashed the greenhouse with stones, then thrown his orchid bulbs into the fish pond. Through the window her body had looked green in the underwater light streaming from the pond. How glorious it must have felt, running half-naked to the greenhouse, gathering up those fleshy cattleya rhizomes, pitching them into the pool. How masterful he must have felt, pushing her through the front door, throwing the bolts. It must have felt, at those moments, as though they had shucked their skins and become lean as knives, cutting open the fabric of their middle-aged lives, letting in the cold air from another place. And wild, too— wild, wild, wild, wild. A frenzy of abandonment.

Or not quite abandonment—because there had always

been little Kaye to consider, even in the throes of relinquishment. They never forgot she was there, lean figure watching at the window or sitting at the table, small but essential audience of one. Take her away and for whom would they perform? She had been the small dark eye to which everything was attuned.

It was only at the very height of their drama that they forgot her completely, in those moments of crisis when they went right to the top of their range, as though performing some magnificent aria, then found each other again, Margaret pounding his chest, Giles pushing at her—then before you knew it they were in the bedroom. Kaye would lie on her bed, listening to the sounds from the other side of the house. She was a sliver now—thin as a bit of darkness. Put it inside.

Later that night, her mother would knock softly on the bedroom door. Kaye kept her face to the wall, though she felt her mother wafting across the room in her nightgown. *Kaye, honey,* she whispered, stroking Kaye's back. *Look at me, please.* Margaret murmured all sorts of things while Kaye stared at the wood grain of the wall, things about life being complicated and marriages hard. She stroked Kaye's back, trying to get her to release the sliver.

But she wouldn't.

Never.

Ah, but turn the image.

Turn it and look at it from a different angle—with all the light of this October day pouring through it. And what you saw was the two of them, father and mother, Zeus and Hera, reconciled; and not by words—by something else. Years passed. Wounds healed. Perhaps—here Kaye had to stop, staring out at the gold leaves—perhaps those wounds had healed not in spite of the fights, but because of them. Or perhaps this was simply what life did to you: it released you whether you wanted release or not.

Whatever had happened, her parents now sailed up the coast every summer, laughing, happy, their boat weighed down with antipasto and frozen steaks—and gold. Laden with so much gold that the hull could barely rise above the water.

Kaye breathed in deeply, her lungs full of bright air.

Six months later she will remember this moment: the light bouncing from the garage, the clear sky, the smell of frost on the grass. She will think about it a lot, remembering the brightness under her ribs, her urge to laugh out loud at the strange resolution of things. Six months later she will stare at the memory, turning its facets a fraction of an inch, trying to see whether, embedded inside, like a seed, she knew what would happen next.

What she will see is herself closing the back door, then lightly passing from room to room, picking up shirts and dirty underwear, stuffing them into the laundry hamper. Six months later she has pulled the scene apart enough times to know what was underneath. It was something that had happened two nights before, as they did the dishes. Daniel suddenly down on his knees, kissing the seam—the thigh seam—of her jeans. It had been so strange at the time, not something she could think about all in one piece. It wasn't the kind of thing they did—not in the kitchen, while they loaded the dishwasher, with Sarah in the next room doing her homework. Kaye had watched him kneeling on the ground, watched as he mouthed at the seam of her jeans, like a horse pushing its big lips at a salt lick. At the time, she had been embarrassed, afraid that the seam might taste salty, had even wanted him to stop. Yet at the same time, it had cracked her open to see him kneeling there, rooting at her with such determination. It had hurt to look down at his head.

Kaye left the house and walked briskly along the street to the bus stop. Between the maple trees she could see a freighter in the harbour, an optical illusion making it seem to float above the water. Beyond the inlet were the pink and grey apartment buildings of West Vancouver, then the newly scoured hillside with all sorts of expensive houses, which looked as though a heavy rain˙could rinse them away. Beyond them the mountains stretched out towards the north, nothing but trees (and hidden clear-cuts) and more trees (and more clear-cuts) all the way to Prince Rupert, and beyond that to Alaska, then the North Pole.

There were clues to what would happen next even as she stepped onto the bus, in her tasselled shoes and tartan skirt. The future was there, sitting just underneath the present, making a bulge like pressure on an eardrum.

At her lunch break she nipped across to the Bay to pick up a rugby shirt for Sarah. Standing in line, she began to think about what had happened after the kitchen scene, after Sarah was in bed. How Daniel had undressed her—small black jeans, white T-shirt—then had her lie on the living-room floor, pinning down her arms. Slowly he had teased her, until she had writhed and snapped at him, acting, but also feeling, a mounting, almost insatiable, lust. Acting, but feeling too—that was strange. Also how he had played with her, holding her down, releasing parts of her neither of them had ever seen. Had that really been herself—calm, reasonable Kaye? Had that man really been Daniel?

She bought the shirt quickly and headed downstairs, into a lingerie shop in the mall, a place she usually never went. It felt illicit, full of red bras, G-strings, foaming pink baby-doll nightgowns. She went to the back of the store, where the lingerie was more risqué: see-through teddies with matching chiffon panties, bras with laces between the cups. She pulled back the padded hangers and looked at a row of corsets. Some were lace, with red fabric roses between the cups. One was black leather with some feathers at the bodice, bone ribbing in the front panels, and under-wire. It had a large zipper down the front and another, smaller one, at the crotch. It reminded Kaye of a Corvette. A man on top of a woman wearing that thing could really feel as though he was mounting his car.

But she took it from its hanger. Yes, she did. And a woman in her late fifties swooped down and took the corset from Kaye and carried it across her arm to the back of the store. She hung it in the change room, stepped back so that Kaye could enter, then pulled the curtains shut with a disturbing clatter of curtain rings, like many, many bangles on an arm.

You are alone, Kaye, with twenty-five minutes left in your lunch break.

She undoes the pearl buttons on her sweater and takes it off. Then comes her cotton sports bra, which looks far past its prime in the yellow light. Her breasts have always been small, as though, at the root, they too are in rebellion. She reaches for the thing, which now seems so absurdly shaped that she wants to laugh out loud. It is moulded to match curves and bulges that are, in turn, supposed to be there. *Doesn't matter,* she tells herself. *Put it on anyway.*

Her skirt bunches on the floor at her feet. She takes the corset and wriggles into it, yanking at the bodice, bouncing up and down.

Once on, it creates an amazing transformation. She sees this at once: it pulls in her stomach, pushes out her buttocks. All she needs is something to stuff the cups with, and some burgundy nail polish.

But why burgundy, Kaye?

Why?

She looks down at her bare fingernails, her thin, boyish hands, surprised, for a moment, that they too haven't changed.

That night Daniel came home three hours late, shaking beads of water from his hair. Sarah was in bed. Kaye sat in the living room, waiting for him, under the glow of the standing lamp, wearing her terry towel robe. They both got bottles of beer, and he picked at the label with his thumbnail. He had been out walking, he said, walking and walking and walking—and now he had to tell her the truth. He said this with a smirk; he couldn't help it. It was the smirk of terrible news: the baby's dead, the cancer has spread. And in the end she couldn't help smirking too—in this moment of burning bridges, of private theatre acted out right there, in the living room.

He began to say what he had done, but slowly, picking again at the beer label. He took so long that she said, *Just stop it and get to the point.* She knew exactly which thin, angry girl he had been fucking even before he told her. Knew too that he would claim that in some reckless way his actions might help them. He would go on about their marriage, talk about lost limbs, things frozen. She watched him: he was bound on a rack. He reached out, took her bony wrist. They both looked down at it; then she pulled it back.

So much of what was to happen to them was there, in that moment. Her silence, her stillness, her refusal to break. Even her insistence, in the days to come, on following a process, never speaking hastily, always ensuring Sarah was out of the house before the subject could be broached. Adherence to a process! Now that had been a gift from the gods themselves, or from her guardian spirit—that skinny black-haired boy in her who knew exactly where to insert the knife. Following respectful processes, facilitating resolutions, all those careful, cold rules she insisted upon—they were just like whispering the word *death* over and over, close to his ear.

Yes, everything was there in that instant, even the fact that eventually, after weeks, after months, she would have to ask forgiveness, first of Daniel and then, finally, of Sarah. This would be much later, when she had cleaved and cracked and broken open.

I'm sorry I didn't scream and throw a plate at the wall.

I'm sorry I tried to break this house on the wheel of my anger.

But for now she stares down at her wrist, where he had touched her. Then she rises from the couch, glassy-eyed, refusing to cry; refusing the slapping, bucking, open-ing, closing moment; refusing the drama. Leaving Daniel waiting for her reaction, she walks from the room and down the hallway to her daughter's bedroom. Kaye lies down beside Sarah, staring past her shoulder at a poster of a black horse with a blaze between its eyes. She can feel that old presence floating near the ceiling, then bending close, a large body wanting to enfold a smaller one. *Talk to me, Kaye.* But no—Kaye is determined to oppose this thing at the root, break change itself in half. And the precise icon of her rage, its essential talisman, is that under her terry towel robe, like a second skin—but vestigial and feathered and only half formed—she is wearing the black corset.

bats

BETH, THAT DARK, shaggy-maned creature, is sitting on the couch, watching me as I cook dinner, a little smile on her lips. *Beth*. A woman with elegant shin bones and beautiful feet. She has a second toe longer than her big toe, a sign, I have read, of poignant insight in those so endowed. (An excellent example of this type of extrasensory foot can be seen in the figure of Venus, in Botticelli's famous *Primavera*.)

My lovely-toed Beth glances up at me and smiles.

She is balancing a glass of red wine on her palm, and turning it, something I believe to be quite risky—but to say so would affect the mood.

"What?" I say. "What's so funny?"

I am peeling the darkly veined bodies of shrimp, making a neat pile of the shells.

"I'm seeing," she says, "if I can make you blush."

I can turn red at a murmur—and of course do so now, on cue. Beth smiles her sibylline smile at this, and I shake a prawn at her, a large one, still in its shell.

We eat our dinner more silently than I had expected. Prawns in Pernod. They have a licorice taste, and seem to cleanse the mouth with each bite, like toothpaste. There is a large, pointed moon outside, one end tipped toward the elm tree. My eyes keep returning to it as I do the dishes. I can feel Beth moving like a sigh behind me, clearing the table and counter, scraping the shells into the garbage can. I like the way she pushes the trash down with the serving spoon to make room for all the shells.

After doing the dishes, we move to the living room and sit on the couch, drinking Frangelico from green liqueur glasses. I want to cradle those coveted toes in the palm of my hand.

"Brendan," she says. Her hair next to my face is soft, almost downy. "Do you have any major fears?"

"Major fears?"

"Phobias."

Aha. Here it is, about to be extended to me, a piece of the Beth puzzle. And I am ready to receive it.

"You have a fear, Beth," I say, reaching out to stroke that absurdly soft hair. "Tell me what it is."

"You tell me first."

"I don't have any."

She swivels to face me, drawing herself to her full height on that long, sensuous spine. Dancers can alter in an instant, I've noticed, changing from supplicating, Beth-like creatures into Madams of the dance, sitting tremendously straight, pointers in hand.

"You *must* have fears," she says.

"But I don't."

"Fear of death."

"Oh that. Well, yes."

"And what about the fear of falling out of an airplane and spinning through the air."

"It's not an ongoing fear, Beth."

She sits back again.

"Now tell me yours," I say, as gently as I can muster.

"I will," she says. "Don't worry."

And she does, next time I see her.

We have bought groceries together in the Japanese specialty store not far from my condominium—strips of nori, crab sticks, raw purple tuna—all for a meal we will cook together (Beth's suggestion). We are standing in the hallway, burdened with groceries, and I am reaching for the keys in the front pocket of my trousers.

"Bats," she says, as though waiting for this precise, perfect moment.

"Which means?"

"You wanted to know my biggest fear. So that's what

it is. Here, let me help you." She reaches a hand into my pants' pocket, finds the keys and draws them out. Her fingers (I haven't mentioned this yet) are cold and long and thin—equine, like her shin bones. Equine, yes, because if a horse could have fingers, it would have Beth's—with her solid knuckles, hard nails, tapering, delicious tips.

Alone, I think of everything I am afraid of.

I'm afraid of deep water, because that's where my father drowned; and I'm afraid of any mention of him; and of white skin, especially when it's wet; I'm afraid (or could be, if I let myself) of cats, and hate their long hair, which makes me sneeze, and possibly stop breathing, turn blue and die; I'm afraid of the gentle winds that carry grief, like the smell of wool socks—part mist, part earth, part sea; I'm afraid of playing catch with my brother and then recalling how we used to do this in the backyard, feeling the burden of memory shudder and fall open; I'm afraid of being the person I'm becoming, especially when I catch a glimpse of myself in the mirror at the gym (where did my hair go?) and see my mouth with its early signs of caving—see, in nascent form, a toothless hole; I'm afraid of children— afraid their yells would fill this stillness and set me on a messy shoal I never dreamed of; but I'm afraid of denying myself intimacy of the type that John (my brother) and his wife, Clarisse, have; I'm afraid of the need that wakes me at night, like something passing over me, a hot breath, a thick, different air—like the touch of a woman's nightgown on my face—leaving me choked with longing.

You can make an art of forgetting. Of holding something in the dark, feeling its contours with your fingers, never naming it.

I brush my teeth, then floss, watching my open mouth in the mirror. Dexterous scraping away of plaque. I drink a large glass of cold water from the fridge. Then I go to bed.

I am in love with Beth.
I am in love with her.
A mistake.

I am in love with Beth. Like one of those Cavalier poets who composed odes to women's eyebrows, I want to write a poem about her childish hair, her toes, her interesting, afflicted knee bones. I want to write about Night. About Beth, at night, being in another part of the city, stretching, rolling, dancing across a floor—or limbering up at the barre in colourful tights cut off at the ankles. I want to write about her feet getting gritty with resin. Gold, soft, crumbling resin.

I want to get close enough to her that I can enter that ring of dark self she emanates, the Beth-aura, twelve inches from her body. Slip inside that. That's what I want.

What is Beth short for, that's what I want to know. Elizabeth? Bethany? Bethsheba?

I am un-careful. I am un-done.

I do things I don't usually do. I say her name out loud to my brother and his wife. The children are running around, from the kitchen into the living room, then through the kitchen again, where we are sitting, finishing our wine after dinner. Their running doesn't bother me: it's characteristic of this house and all its artful chaos, its births and screaming and kids and cats.

My brother and sister-in-law watch me. Do they notice the dark bubble I am carrying inside me—this need I have to say her name? I do it as unobtrusively as I can. Out it comes, as potent as a small moment of death, a flutter like the soft, powdered wings of a moth.

Mossy, dark name.

Secret urn.

Beth.

They look at each other. They laugh. Children rush through the room. Clarisse raises her head and bellows—*Hey, stop it!*—a sudden foghorn. She is a petite woman, Clarisse, delicately laughing at my blush, then transforming in an instant into a foghorn. I feel that she should give a warning, the way they do on ferries.

My brother is trying not to smile. He looks away.

"Is she nice?" Clarisse asks.

More blushing.

"She seems nice. Yes, I would say she seems nice."

"What does she do?" That's my brother. Checking her assets.

"She's a dancer, actually."

"Oh, Brendan!" Clarisse reaches out, puts her hand on my arm, holding on to me as though I'm already gone—ridiculously adrift, perhaps even about to be shipwrecked.

"And she teaches fitness," I say.

Ah, that makes more sense: fitness instructors are part of our world. But it's too late, anyway. I've given myself away.

I shouldn't have told them. It takes an entire day and a night to get over my brother's ruthless conviviality. A day to submerge his gross conceptions, to let the shadows grow large again. A full day, and then a night. That's what my brother can do to me with just one remark: *Building a relationship isn't easy, you know.* He makes it sound like building a solid brick structure. A Bank of Commerce, for instance.

Now all that's left is the conclusion.

Sad Beth. Short for Bethany.

We lie in bed—new Beth, penetrated Beth, *known* Beth, and I. We lie together, rather sleepily, trying to get comfortable. Her legs, which go on and on for miles when stretched on couches or grapevining across the fitness-room floor, are harder to accommodate, neatly, in my bed. Just as we jostle our way to a respectable accommodation, she lets her mouth venture to my ear, breath sharp with the consumption of raw tuna, and says one word. One sleepy word.

"Bats."

Then: "My phobia," she says. "Need to tell you."

"Phobia," I say. "That's from *phobos,* the Greek for *fear.*"

She turns away, soft hair brushing my cheek. I stare at her back, its delicate knobs of bone, her shoulder blades, which look designed for flight. I kiss her skin, not where a bone lies, but in the space between the tracery of bones. Resting my ear to her back, I hear the murmur of complex machinery, and somewhere, far away, the soft, watery thump of her heart.

"Tell me," I say.

"You don't have to hear about it if you don't want to."

"But I do want to."

"Well," she says at last. "I didn't know what to do. Then a friend of mine told me about a twelve-step program you can take, for any kind of phobia. It's offered through the Jewish Y. So I took it: a twelve-step program for bat phobia."

She is sitting up now, sheet covering her knees, hair lit by the street lamp outside.

"We started out small, looking at pictures of bats. Talking about the things we didn't like. You know: eyes, teeth, wings, claws. I particularly hated their furry heads. Then we'd draw pictures of what we hated. Or watch a movie about vampires. The instructor talked a lot about what bats *really* are, deep down. I mean, they're just mammals. Warm-blooded. They bear their young in their bodies, you know."

"That helped?"

"I think so. Knowing the truth, staring at the truth, helped. *Pegging it* helped. Then, at the end, we went out— god, I still can't believe this—we actually went out into the ravine, on a dark night, and climbed through the muck until we were right under the viaduct. The instructor shone his flashlight up under the steel frame. There were thousands of bats right there, within touching distance, bunched together. I could see their furry heads. When the beam of light hit them, they froze—bats won't move if you shine a light right at them. Then the instructor reached out, gave a twist, pulled one off and held it in his hand. It was like a baby bird. I mean, this bat was trembling, and I could see its heart beating. Then we put a splash, just the smallest splash, of phosphorescent paint on its stomach. Then the instructor let it go. That one, then another, then another—about twenty in all."

She shakes her head, looking into the darkness in the bedroom.

"It was the most beautiful thing I've ever seen, Brendan. They were like fireflies. Or shooting stars."

She stops speaking then.

"Now tell me what you're afraid of," she says.

She stares down at me in the bed, where I am lying motionless, holding my breath. I can feel her attempting to absorb every nuance of my expression. But still I know that she isn't quite capturing everything she needs to see, and that in another second she will reach out and switch on the bedside light.

levitation

"THERE ARE NO MIRACLES." The doctor announced this fact over breakfast. He was talking to his son, James, but also to their housekeeper, Nell, who lived at the doctor's house and looked after James now that his mother was dead.

It was late March, 1893, in the countryside not far from Waterloo, Ontario. The doctor turned from the table and looked out the window at the rain. It poured steadily down, blurred by a fog at the bottom of the pane. Through the glass he could see the streaked arm of the black walnut tree.

"Every time that mankind has believed in supernatural occurrences," he continued, "miracles if you like, they have turned out to be a product of our own ignorance. The ancients thought that the sun was the god Helios, travelling across the sky in a gold chariot drawn by fiery horses. In fact, we know it's a ball of gas, hydrogen and helium, the mass of which, bearing down on itself, causes a perpetual explosion." This was a bad example, he could see that. There hadn't been any sun for days, only a black and relentless rain. The mud in the yard was rain-clogged, and boards had been laid from the front door to the road.

"Rain," he said. "Primitives used to pray for rain—rain dances, rain chants, water for the crops. Whole deities have sprung up, in Egypt and elsewhere, based on the swelling of the Nile, the desire for fertility. My point, James, is that all these phenomena—the sun, the rain, the stars—they all have scientific explanations. Things function on principles: gravitation, evaporation, the rising and falling of rivers, the natural weight of gases. The entire earth, and the universe for that matter, follows laws. And they're good laws—that's what I mean to say. You'll see that yourself as you get older. They're good laws, good, sensible laws, with a natural dignity—and you don't need any crackpots, miracle workers or mystic seers, or whatever, claiming they can tinker and tamper with them."

James had listened carefully. He had been trying to grab hold of the nut of information his father had given him, to pry it open and get the meat out of it, but it seemed unbreakable, whole unto itself, black and even dry within. Through the sheet of water on the window he saw the slippery mud, slick with promise, a hippopotamus hide. He had sat at the window and pretended such things with his mother—seen faces in the drops, long noses, eyes that wept, horses trickling down the pane. On sunny days he and his mother had seen figures in the clouds too. They had lain on their backs in the garden the summer before she got sick, the earth heavy with the drone of bees, and seen elephants and carriages, a dogsled team and a monkey. She would have laughed wickedly, inciting him to mockery and rebellion, at this speech so full of words like *evaporation*, *gravitation*, *phenomena*. Now he felt her insistence, moving him not to betray her.

"But the magician—and he was a real magician, because why else was everyone there—and you even said I could go see him—"

"I meant for you to enjoy yourself, not to believe every blessed thing."

"He made her rise up. I saw it. We all did. The woman lay down on the table—a table just like this one—and the lights darkened a bit, and she rose up. We all saw—and people all around us clapped, didn't they, Nell?"

"Well," said Nell, "I must say it was impressive, Doctor Flemming. It was very neatly done, I'll say that. Certainly there were no strings you could see. Because he had a lady from the audience come up and check. She ran her hand up and down, around the floating body. I must say it *seemed* very real."

The doctor had had a sense of foreboding about letting Nell take James to the show, but Nell had suggested that it might be good for him, might cheer him up and bring him out of himself. Instead, it had had the reverse effect. There was a knot of belief in the boy, a light in his eyes that was not, strictly speaking, safe. He was holding on to this idea despite the implausibility of it. In fact, the very irrationality seemed to be what was making him believe.

"There weren't strings, Father," he said. "We all saw, didn't we, Nell?"

"It certainly *seemed* that way, James," she said, "but you know how these things work."

"He made her rise up—he made her rise up. We all saw."

"Now hold on, James," his father said. "Nobody can make somebody rise up."

"I saw."

"You were tricked."

"I saw."

The boy grasped his knife in one hand, its blade yellow from the poached egg. With his blond hair cropped in a circle around his head, his face drained of colour, he had the valiant look of a child Saint George. He was like his mother, with his blue, excited eyes, his watery, fine lashes and ears that stuck out from his head, red now with the exertion of rebelling.

"I saw it happen, and afterwards Nell took me back-stage, and the magician, Mr. Boyle, he said I could be good at it too. He said I had the gift."

"Nell, you didn't."

"I didn't see the harm—and the boy was so keen."

The father stared at her—cold as the moon, she thought—then directed his gaze at the boy. "Mr. Horatio Boyle is a quack," he said, "a fraud and a fake. Nell was daft to take you, I was daft to allow it, and you, my boy, are daft if you believe a word of what he said. Now, go and change your shirt, it's filthy with egg."

The boy threw down his knife on the plate, and his father caught his hand.

"Pick it up," he said, "and place it down quietly, where it belongs."

James picked up his knife and placed it on a slant across the plate, then pushed his fork into position also.

"You're too old to believe in hocus-pocus," his father said, but the boy's eyes were hooded now, covert, and he went upstairs without another word.

All winter the land had been comforting and bleak, the stubble of cornstalks covered for six months with snow. No colour in the landscape, or colours that were thin, imperceptible. When the doctor walked to his practice in town, which he did in all but the worst weather, he heard water running under the ice, coming from many places he could not see. But now it was March and the snow had melted. Rain had turned everything to mud.

Spring had also brought a scourge of mystics. They travelled like peddlers from town to town, claiming they had the third eye or could guess the contents of one's pouch. They were the worst kind of falsifiers. Some said they could heal with a laying-on of hands, and some would lead seances in town, so the doctor had heard, but always for a price. Swindlers, the doctor thought as he stared out the window at the slick, wet trunk of the walnut tree.

Nell cleared James's plate and her own and went into the kitchen. The doctor could hear her moving around recklessly, scraping the uneaten egg into a bucket. Let her think he was wrong; it didn't matter. One day, perhaps, his son would thank him for teaching him this bitter capacity to face the truth, for never telling a lie to give false hope, never casting the shadow of illusion over their lives. He was giving James tools, solid as the rigging on ships, with which to rein himself in, to master his impetuosity.

He saw his son's face as it was so often nowadays when he stared out the window at night: shadowed, partially occluded. He needed to drag James back, just as though he had been drowning, and find a way to scour his skin, make the blood flow, rub his body alive, even if it meant causing pain at first. He was like a captain, so he believed; like Captain Bligh, who was severed from those around him, whose men hated him. They put him in a boat in the middle of the Pacific with eighteen loyal men and three days' supply of water, but he brought every one of them back alive. That was how the father saw himself as he broke his yolk with the blade of his knife, alone in the dining room: He could face facts. He could bring them back alive.

But that idea seemed so false, as he heard himself think it, that he could only put down his knife and shake his head, shake it repeatedly at his own capacity for self-deception. She had taken months to die, so long that even now, a year later, he sometimes felt she was still there, upstairs. He had gone back and forth to her room on tip-toe, bringing vegetable broth, which he fed her by dipping a cloth in it, then holding it to her lips.

She was the daughter of a Mennonite farmer, only seventeen when he married her; he had been forty at the time. He used to see her in the fields when he walked to his office in the town. She met his eyes and didn't turn away, didn't even blush. She was like an animal—simply watching. Then one day her father brought her to the doctor's office because she had gashed her arm with a scythe. When he was alone with her, the doctor had trouble speaking. He felt old, and he worried that he smelled of the camphorated oil he used as a night liniment. She pulled back her sleeve and showed him the gash, and he cleaned away the dried blood, then wrapped a bandage around her forearm, closing the red opening of the wound. Later she told him she had cut herself so that she could see him. *I cut myself for you,* she said. Like a fox gnawing itself from a trap.

He could never understand her. Sometimes she seemed like a polluted child, preternaturally knowing. Sometimes she turned her head and smiled at him with radiant innocence. She was happier with James, after he was born, than she had ever been with him, that much he knew, because James just asked and took and cried and sucked, in such an ordinary way; while he had loved her too much, and never in the right way.

As she died, the bones of her cheeks and nose had jutted forward while her flesh receded, until she looked like a grasshopper, an ancient, terrible insect with huge watery eyes and thin fingers that would grasp his wrist. "Sit by me, William," she would say in a clear voice, because death had even picked out all the stray tones. At the very end, sometimes, he had stayed away. "She wants you," Nell would say, while he looked up from the cradle of light he was in, the book opened on his crossed knee. *I cannot get my work done,* he had said, first to himself and then out loud. It made him feel safe, in a gel of self-loathing, to hear himself say this, to see Nell's startled look, her confirmation of what kind of man he really was. He sat and drank his sherry and read Thucydides, then at nine o'clock he went to her room. He had only kept her waiting for an hour.

Now James could be heard out in the hall, getting his school books, putting on his overshoes. The doctor went into the hall and touched the boy's blond hair.

"You have a good day at school," he said. "You work hard. Learn a few things. And I'll be expecting you to tell me what new piece of knowledge you've acquired at the end of the day, so keep that head of yours on tight." He wanted the boy to say something, to look at him, but James turned and ran—out the door, over the bare planks laid across the mud and through the waiting gate.

The air had thickened—that was the first sign. The air around James's eyes had deepened and become full of specks of light. Some were turquoise, like peacocks' tails, and they shifted into cobalt, the colour of the apothecary jars in which his father kept his powders. The heads of the people in front of James darkened. Mr. Horatio Boyle stood on the stage, behind a table, his face bright in the limelight, and everything else was brown; even his eyes were plugs of brown. James heard the magician chanting to his familiar, the spirit of Margaret Barrance. *For no one will rise without the help of those powers that move us, spirits fair and white, and even the planets must be aligned and the hours ready in their turn. Alpha and Omega, Sadonay, Iskyros, Adonay.* James heard a thrumming, and then he was very close to the stage. He could have touched the woman as she lay in the air. He knew her palms were wet. Her skirt hung beneath her, but there was nothing holding her except thickened air. It held her delicately breathing body, while air muttered through her lips. Her eyelids were closed, her face dotted with little blasts of surfaced blood vessels, her mouth slack, her chin nestled in the ripples of her neck. The magician flitted beside her, moving his arms over and under—a shaft of black, a bat's wing, showing, showing, showing, what anyone could see.

At four o'clock that afternoon the rain stopped. The last whip of it spattered James's face as he walked up the road from town, coming home from school. As he walked beside the fence, he heard splashing. The walnut seemed to hold buckets of water high up in its branches, which it released in long slooshes as the wind moved. The country road they lived on, concession road number six, was lit now by the wan sun between the clouds.

James went through the gate and along the wooden walkway that crossed the mud. He lay down on the board under the black walnut tree, where he had lain with his mother two summers before, looking at the leaves, sucking blades of grass, eating the white ends. *I won't stop loving you, James, just because I'm not there. That's not how it works.* That's what his mother had said to him before she died. James looked up at the watery branches, and when he tilted his head back, he saw the line of poplars on the windy side, tall as lighthouses.

At first Nell thought he was dead out there. She just saw the lump of him on the board, in his dun-coloured shirt and dark trousers. She didn't take time to pick her way to him, but bounded across the mud, spoiling her inside shoes, only to find he was gazing at the trees, breathing lightly, not glancing at her but not, on the other hand, really ignoring her either.

"What are you doing?" She put her hands on her waist. "What *exactly* do you think you're doing?"

He did not answer, but gazed instead at the sky. She looked up too and saw the limbs of the tree, the drops clinging to the twigs.

"You'll catch your death of cold," she said. He seemed to be muttering something under his breath. She watched. Was he counting? His shirt sleeve had touched the mud, and she had the bad feel of it on her mind. The cloth was wicking the mud in, and she could imagine how cold his body must be getting.

"Now look here, James. You must, absolutely must, get up—and here's my promise: if you get up now, I'll tell your father nothing about it. How's that, eh? Only you must get up now and come into the house."

His teeth weren't chattering, not yet. But his lips were moving. She leaned in close and watched his mouth. *Sadonay,* his lips formed, *Iskyros, Adonay, Saboath.*

"James," she cried. "Stop that. That's not a good thing to do."

Tetragrammaton, Emanuel, sether, pantos, cratons, alpha and omega, and all other names in which you show yourself, fearful and true. Show.

She felt the long slant of the trees, and the empty house, its windows unopened. She had the sense of a face waiting at the window. It sent a shiver running up her spine.

I command thee by the virtue of our Lord. I command thee by the virtue of his uprising and by the virtue of his flesh and body that he took of the Blessed Virgin Mary. Raise me.

"Get up," she said. "You're scaring me."

She wanted help but would not run across the fields to her sister's house. Something pressed close by, and if she left the boy, she might come back to find him strung vertical, a shaft of black under the tree. She looked around wildly and screamed—for there was the doctor, gaunt as a pole by the garden gate, his face stony with anger and old blame.

"What are you doing, Nell?"

"It's not me, Doctor. I'm trying to stop him."

"What is he doing?"

"I don't know. I don't know."

"James," said his father. "What are you doing? Get up."

Nell could feel James concentrate even harder on the words, which he mouthed without sound, looking at the sky. His father came through the gate and stood at his son's feet, looking at his lips.

"Those are the words the magician taught him, aren't they?"

"Yes, sir."

The father knelt on one knee, not touching his son

43

but listening, as doctors do. Then he stood up and rubbed his mouth with his palm, back and forth, looking up at the sky. "I'm not going to argue with you," he said softly. "I'm not going to force you. I'm going to leave you here, and you are going to learn."

The boy pressed himself harder into his spell. That caused the doctor to draw in his breath, as though biting down on something cold. "You will see," he said. "You will stay here until doomsday and you won't move an inch. Now come in, Nell, and leave him." He walked up the board to the house and closed the door behind him.

In his bedroom, the doctor took off his shirt, trousers and coat and hung them on the hook behind the cupboard door. He changed and went to the window. Nell was still crouched on her knees, remonstrating, insisting, while his son stared up at the tree. When the doctor came downstairs in his slippers, Nell was in the kitchen, mud on the hem of her skirt. She was waiting to speak, but he passed through like a ship that must keep going, past the deadheads and dark promontories, fed by a small light in its bow. He poured himself his sherry and went through to the parlour. When Nell appeared at the door, he glanced up with that mixture of loathing and humour he reserved particularly for her.

"You can't leave him," she said. "He's doing this for you, you know."

"I have no idea what he's doing it for. But I have no intention of doing anything."

"He's cold as a bone."

"Then let him come inside."

"At least let me bring him a blanket."

"Don't you think you've meddled enough?"

"Me!" She stood back as if her face had been slapped.

"Feeding his head with nonsense—magicians, levitations. I can't think what more you could do."

She stood balanced on one foot, feeling both insulted and hideously stupid, then she went to the larder and brought out the pickled eggs, which she placed in a bowl. She laid out the cold chicken on a platter and placed the eggs and chicken on the kitchen table. That was all the preparation she was capable of.

They sat and ate together while the boy lay outside, in the dusk. She could see him through the window, stretched out on the ground, his face gleaming white beside the puddles. It frightened her—but not as much as the face of the doctor. He cut his chicken meticulously, his eyes hooded, brought each portion to his mouth and chewed thoroughly. When dinner was over, and the doctor told her she could go, Nell ran out the back door. James was still there, in the same position, but his eyes had an unbelieving look in them now, of ice and sadness.

"Oh James," Nell said, "don't you see it's not working." But he would not move. "I'm going to get help," she whispered. "I'm going to my sister's."

As she ran across the field, she was frightened by what was happening, what she had left.

Iskyros. Sadonay. Spirit white and fair. Show.

The air was thickening in the poplars. Coins of light gabbled against each other high up in the branches, but it was only the wind moving the leaves. The board beneath James's back was cold, his shoulders ached, but a weight heavier than his body pressed him down. James saw the house, felt the density of it, the weight of the sky and the empty walnut tree. If he had tried to move, he couldn't have stood up. If he had been able to, he would have turned himself into mud.

He stopped the meaningless chanting.

Inside, his father stood at the window. The yard had turned mauve in the setting sun, and night was rising out of the ground. His son lay beneath the tree, his shirt and face carrying the gleam of a shroud. His body was a reproach, a black slice aimed at his father, for failing, for letting her die.

The doctor held the sill and closed his eyes. He could smell the warm grass and milk of her, and feel the heat of her hand against the pain in his side. *I wanted you so much,* he thought, *I wanted you,* and he felt her there all over again, a rush of warmth—up through his chest, down his arms—a single laugh that he would think it was too late.

He opened his eyes and went to the door.

James saw the square of light on the mud, and his father, a stab of darkness against the door frame, a shadow moving along the board, quickly, too quickly—then stepping off the board into the mud. He saw his father's face near his own, struggling to contain the warmth that was breaking in him. *I should have come sooner,* the father wanted to say, *I was always there, I always meant to come,* but instead he knelt in the mud, placed one arm under his son's neck, the other under his knees, and lifted him up.

annunciation

IN THIS PLACE THE SUN IS A RUMOUR. It is useless to have eyes. Open them. All you see is blackness. Velvet blackness. Total blackness. But wait, there is a whisper of green, a moving filament, a worm of light. It comes from inside a bioluminescent jellyfish, its sheath of eggs streaming behind it, encased in bubbles. Up and down the creature floats, trailing luminescence, waving hair-thin feelers, giving off blips of life . . .

Amanda woke. At first she didn't know where she was. Existence itself seemed peculiar, as though she had squeezed back into her life through the eye of a needle. She was staring across the room at a mirror, very large and gilt-framed, which indicated something about who she was, but in a kind of code, like Egyptian hieroglyphics. Then she remembered that it was Simon's mirror.

But where had she been, that was the question. And what had she dreamt? She woke waterlogged, as though her body had floated for three days and then been cast up on a beach, already nibbled by fish, worried open. Then her life murmured and took shape, poured back and filled her until it was everything—everything that was and everything that could be—and the other thing was gone.

Amanda stretched, sat up and put her feet out of the bed, her naked body reflected in the mirror. At twenty-two she was at the peak of her bloom, the period of maximum growth before decay. She was dewy and fresh, with a down on her skin like a peach. It made people want to reach out and stroke her, even smell her. Her blond hair fell in soft tresses, like the hair of Simonetta Vespucci, the model Botticelli used for his most famous paintings. And her face too was like one of his heavy-lidded Madonnas, or Venus riding the shell, dawn covering her skin with unawareness, like the skin of a birch, blue in the snow, before morning. That was the kind of beauty Amanda Melanchuk had.

Still, she also had the kind of body that would definitely gather flesh with age, packing fat on the breasts, shoulders, stomach—becoming transformed, as her own mother had been transformed with time. Amanda had heard Simon say that her mother had the figure of a missile silo, and it was true. She was uniformly fat all over, narrowing only at the head.

Simon and Amanda lived in an apartment in a

medical-dental building on the west side of Toronto. To get to their apartment they had to walk through an antiseptic lobby with a drugstore at one end. It smelled of bandages, fluoride, medical disinfectant. Up above, on the seventh floor, they had a view of Roncesvalles Avenue. Looking south, beyond the six lanes of the freeway, they could see the body of Lake Ontario. It was calm most of the time, as though brooding on its failure, despite its enormous size, to generate enough action to have tides. Amanda could feel its presence all the time; just as, lying in bed or standing at the window, she could feel the movements of people in the rooms around her, slashes and trails of darkness, moving from kitchen to bathroom to living room. She was fond of these people who surrounded her invisibly: the old couple who lived above her, the girl and her father who lived on the fourth floor and whom Amanda often met in the elevator as she left for work. The girl was small, sallow, wearing the same blouse every day, and a tartan skirt with a green parrot appliquéd onto it, very bright, like another kingdom. Her father's name was Joe Dunn. He had introduced himself.

Beside her in the bed, Simon had curled into a fetal position, the down pillow between his legs. In the half dark she could see the knobs of his backbone. His hair on the pillow was rough from bleach, spiky from old gel. His face was turned away, but she knew that if she leaned over, peered into the dark to read his features, he would look pained. She looked down at him with a mixture of alarm and maternal possession. She wondered at his tenacious ability to hold on to sleep—through the alarm, the garbage trucks, her soft breath on his face.

She wrapped herself in her robe and picked her way through the sea of his accretions toward the bathroom. Simon collected things, pasted them to other things—glued, fastened, melted, remoulded, re-glued, photographed, burnt, resurrected; and out of these transmogrifications came an art that sold occasionally. She passed a table spray-painted silver and covered in Barbie shoes, plastic dinosaurs and shards of broken crockery. A chandelier hung from the living-room ceiling. It was made of a skirt hoop, like a cage, studded with artificial pearls, diamonds and GI Joe action figures.

In the bathroom Amanda performed her ablutions, standing in the shower, letting the hot water spray over her face, then turning to warm the small of her back. She washed herself with a bar of green soap—under her arms, under her breasts, sitting down on the side of the tub to move the soap bar between her toes, getting into the cracks and crannies as though washing a hard-to-clean teapot, scouring as much as she could of the inside, getting under folds, into nooks and spouts. This was important. Not that being thoroughly clean was so very crucial in and of itself; it was more what it would mean if she allowed herself to be dirty. She was the type, she knew, from whom rowdy, inexplicable smells could arise. Pheromones. If she wasn't vigilant, these embarrassing, feral scents would leach from her as insistently as the hair grew back on her legs.

When she went back to the bedroom, Simon was finally awake, lying on his back, staring at the ceiling.

"You're up," she said.

"Not even close." He shut his eyes. He looked like a wax figure, a dead medieval youth. He opened his eyes, turned on one side, and watched as she opened the mirrored closet and began to select her clothes, which she kept clean and ironed.

"Could you do me a small favour?" he said.

She nodded.

"Could you go to the window and give the blinds a turn, so that the light comes in in stripes?"

She went and fiddled with the wand attached to the blinds. "Like that?"

"Yes, that's good."

He leaned on one elbow and watched her dress in the slats of light—her perfect knees, round haunches, the shadows under her breasts. There were gradations of yellow in her skin, and some blue bouncing back from the mirror, causing a contrast, an introduction of a sombre hue. She gathered her clothes from the chair—stockings, polyester trousers, blazer—preparing to carry them away.

"What are you doing?"

"You know it makes me nervous when you watch me."

"I can't help it. Besides," he said, "I'm not really watching you. I'm looking at your skin, I'm looking at its shades."

It was an impasse: if she left, she would hurt him, albeit only minorly, but if she got dressed right there in front of him, she would feel miserable herself.

"All right," she said. "But if you're going to watch, then don't narrow your eyes. I hate that."

"Narrow my eyes?"

"Like you're measuring me."

He lay back and laughed. Whatever she said, even at her angriest, never seemed to do anything but delight him, as though it was another example of *something*—some precocious simplicity she exhibited merely by being herself.

"All right," he agreed. "I'll watch you exactly as you like to be watched. Which is?"

She was pulling on her nylons, one foot on the bed, and she paused, thinking about this. "As though you're my fiancé," she said at last.

"Which I am."

"Which you are."

But he was never quite how she wanted him. He always played his part too cheerfully, with a wink at the audience, as though being a fiancé was the most pleasurable lark in the world. And meanwhile Amanda was just trying, every day, and very hard, to make things work out the way she had pictured them in her head. But then again, if she had really wanted things to work out in the proper way, the Melanchuk way, would she have chosen Simon as the man to marry? No. She would have chosen a manager of a butcher shop, someone who spent all day among frozen cuts of beef, or a young lawyer, someone with a really good chin who would take her for cocktails after work.

She had thwarted her best interests from the beginning, but what could she do? It was Simon who interested her—Simon with his concave chest, like the guy who got sand kicked in his face before he started bodybuilding; Simon who was so lean she sometimes felt she could see into his bones.

It was he who had suggested they move in together. Her roommate had moved out, and Simon was over all the time. They had been sitting on her balcony when he asked her, on a sunny day the previous September. The woman in the apartment next door was out watering her plants, wearing a long quilted muumuu. Amanda watched her moving between her plants, holding the plastic watering can.

"I've always wanted—" Amanda had said at last. "I mean, I've always thought... that when I moved in with a man, or he moved in with me, it would be because we were married."

Simon threw back his head and laughed. But when he saw her hurt reaction, he reached out his hand. "You're amazing," he said. "How do you do it? My god, Amanda, we live in an age that's blasted with debris and dead rot and garbage—but you sail on, all in one piece. You are the most amazing person. You *adhere*." He said this last word as though it were the greatest compliment in the world.

Then all at once he had knelt in front of her deck chair, sweeping his bleached hair impatiently back with all the fingers of one hand. He was voluptuously thin and lean and loose-limbed, and as he knelt, she saw, overprinted, a courtly eighteenth-century paramour with a tricorn hat and velvet breeches, a ruffled shirt and brocade waistcoat. He was both dashing and boyish, ardent and wounded, cold and hot—and he was offering her his hand.

"Yes," she whispered. "Yes, I'll marry you." She raised his head up to the warm, powdered centre between her breasts, and pressed it there.

Simon had thrown himself into the preparations for the wedding with a verve that overwhelmed Amanda. And how could she tell him, when he was so obviously excited—sketching designs for the wedding dress himself, ordering the flowers—how could she tell him that his attitude wasn't quite what she desired? Before he proposed, Amanda had worried from time to time that Simon wouldn't care about getting married. Never in her wildest imaginings had she worried that he would enjoy it too much.

"I want layers of taffeta," he said, showing her pictures of wedding gowns in bridal magazines. "And lace down the back, and a bow, here—they call it in French the *parfait contentement*—to show off that magnificent bosom. And a train, we need something spangled with a dust of opal sequins. And I've been toying, just toying, with the concept of panniers to flush out the silhouette, to give it size."

Amanda felt a sinking sensation when she looked at the pictures. It was going to be Simon's gown, not hers. I don't want all this, she thought, but it was too late: they were in the midst of something big—something she thought of as The Wedding Show. Once it's over, everything will be all right, she told herself; but increasingly she felt that the thing she had to swallow was inordinate—like being forced, single-handedly, to eat an octopus.

There are places that do not seem to want to exist. That was what the land was like along the 401, to and from Purlex Plastics, where Amanda worked. It was the edge of Toronto—part farmland, part corporate sprawl—and there was a casual ugliness to the concrete bridges and overpasses, the power poles and big-box furniture outlets.

Once, it had been grassland. Once, birds had swarmed here by the thousands, filling the sky. But even then the land may have caused a mild choking sensation. Perhaps the place was haunted, the bog gases holding the weight of dead animals in them, their spirits oppressing the air.

Amanda parked her red Dodge Colt at the far end of the parking lot. The corporate and manufacturing headquarters of Purlex Plastics rose in front of her, a building three storeys tall covered in white vinyl sheeting.

Purlex made almost everything: walls, doors, blinds, door frames, baby toys, plastic wrap, intravenous bags, pipes, credit cards, picket fences. They started with salt, chlorine and ethylene chrysalis, mixed in plasticizers—DEHP, Bi-Phenol A—then fire retardants, stabilizers, colourants. Finally, the stable vinyl was laid out in long sheets and cut into the desired shapes. This process took place in the depths of the extrusion plant. Amanda, who had a job in Control and Ordering, had never seen the mixing or the bonding of the plastics.

This morning the white Purlex building was moody against the grey sky, full of a soft foreboding. Often, as Amanda walked toward the building, she felt something tease her mind from far away, an ancient memory across vegetable existence, across a life—a shuddering, encompassing sense edged in the finest sheen. Yet when she tried to meet her thought—when she glanced up at the building feeling the gathering force of the message—it died away.

How could she explain this? She couldn't explain it to anyone.

It made her feel bathed in significance, quite against her own will. Sometimes she entered the building with her face flushed, her palms sweating.

Ten o'clock.

A time of languor in the extrusion headquarters. Myra was already nibbling at her tuna sandwich—spongy white bread with a sad bit of iceberg lettuce poked between the slices. The large room was divided into several work clusters, each with two women at it. This allowed the staff to move about easily, gathering and dispersing materials, while being watched from the side office by Mr. Kyle. All around her Myra heard the slither of nylon stockings, the tap of coloured nails on keyboards.

Myra bent over the computer printout on her desk, checking numbers against those on her screen, circling inventory that was getting low: phalates for hardening the vinyl, Bi-Phenol A for softening. She drummed her blood-red nails on the desktop and glanced at Amanda, a shaft of ill will. It seemed to Myra that the hardest aspect of her already hard-to-bear existence was having to share a work-station with Amanda, the goddess of flesh and perfect idiocy. There she sat: dressed appropriately, combed and coiffed, eager to please. Myra scowled. Briefly she imagined pushing Amanda against a wall, pressing her own taut, angry torso against Amanda's full breasts.

Myra turned away, irritated, and took a sip of her coffee. It tasted nauseating. It was possible, she was realizing, distinctly possible that her idiotic body was pregnant. Her lover, a married university professor, was going to have trouble with that one. The idea sent a wave of heat from her face to her calves. She put her fingernails to her temples and muttered a word her therapist had suggested she make up to calm her nerves, a secret word known only to herself. *Eloj,* she whispered. *Eloj.*

"So," she said after a while, turning to Amanda, "where's your friend?"

"What?"

"Where's your friend?" She jerked her head, and Amanda looked over at the window of their supervisor, Mr. Gerald Kyle, head of shipments and ordering. She saw his shadow behind the misted glass, moving like a shark in a tank, making furtive darts and jabs as he paced and talked on the telephone.

"Isn't this when he usually pops his head out to say a special hello?"

Amanda looked at Myra's cropped, gelled hair, the skeletal, heart-shaped face and freckled skin. Myra's freckles extended to her arms and hands, giving the impression that she was covered all over with a light dotting, like a deer hide. Under this covering Amanda saw a trapped boy, ravenous and ill intentioned.

"He's not my friend."

"No? Tell that to him."

Amanda continued to check her printout. There were columns and columns of phalates on the printout, and they were all, at least on the first several pages, phalate-b's.

Mr. Kyle opened his door and entered the central area, the grave look on his face masking his anticipated pleasure. The women in ordering and shipping were like his harem, though they smelled of raspberry lip gloss and kiwi hair gel instead of jasmine or sandalwood. And if they were his harem, then Amanda—Amanda was his white odalisque.

Mr. Gerald Kyle was a man so obviously shaped by his sexual cravings, that it was hard to glance at the most innocent part of him (his heavily pored nose, for instance, or the back of his neck with its basset hound folds, or his ring finger with its purple-jewelled engineering ring) without thinking, simultaneously, of his penis.

He went from workstation to workstation, ruler in hand, thwacking it lightly on his palm as he checked the printouts. When he came to Amanda's desk, she felt a sudden cessation of movement behind her. She was seated on one of the new ergonomic chairs, with a metal spine and small padded seat that rather alarmingly exposed her rear end to public view. Heat rose in the clammy space between her legs, beneath her pantyhose.

"How's it coming, Amanda?" He stood near her, just inside the aura she gave off—deodorant and L'Air du Temps Eau de Cologne.

"I marked the fluctuations, at least the most noticeable ones." She pointed to the red marks on the printout.

"That's helpful."

As his eyes flicked over her, she felt an itch on her ankle—a bad itch, like the rising of a welt. She glanced down, expecting to see a small cluster of blisters. They were an occupational hazard of the workplace. Almost all of the girls had had them at one time or another, and management had changed the carpet twice because of them. But no, her ankles were smooth.

Nevertheless, she reached out and scratched her ankle, once, hard.

"Is something wrong?" Mr. Kyle asked. "Are you having a reaction?"

"It's nothing."

"A weal?"

"No, I don't think so."

"You sure you don't want me to look?"

"It's nothing at all. Really." She met his eyes and felt a

small electric shock. He seemed to have grown out of the atmosphere, to seep from it, so that his clothes had the same seminal reek as the carpet. It made her tonsils ache. But his eyes—they were electric. She had seen a lamprey eel in an aquarium once, and it looked just like Mr. Kyle.

"Come see me tomorrow at this time," he said. "I need your help to check the stockroom."

As he walked away, she heard the vindictive hum of the women. *Don't put up with it. Report it to management. Stockroom, I bet.*

"You don't need to put up with that shit," Myra whispered when he was gone.

"He just wants to give me an assignment." Amanda was angry too—angry at Gerald Kyle for singling her out, angry at herself for the blush that had covered her face and then receded, leaving her cheeks blotchy.

Myra let her eyes flick down to Amanda's breasts, then up again. "It's verging on sexual harassment," Myra whispered.

"I don't know," Amanda said.

"Well, I do."

But what was happening to her? She rubbed the smooth skin of her ankle bones again.

"I'll be back," she said, and went down the hall to the

washroom. In the mirror she looked more or less like who she was: the same blond hair, the same lyrical face, which seemed oddly beautiful even to herself. She saw her face as something flagrant and damaging—a mark or blessing for which she had been unprepared. The first time Simon showed her his book on the Uffizi, she recognized herself in pictures of the Madonna—the golden-haired one in the courtyard, watching an ant cross the dry and patterned rock, then looking up to see the angel with the face of a lion. He does not speak; the words come from his forehead. *But I am not ready,* the Madonna wants to say. She thinks of the ant, the sickle-shaped crumb of bread in its jaws. But a message burns from the angel's brown, lined forehead, and there is no shadow left in the courtyard to say, *Why me?* No honour or fear. Then he flies into the sunbeam and is gone; the long beam, mote streaming, bakes her with radiance; and her head and feet tingle with light.

Amanda combed her hair slowly, then sat down in a cubicle with the door closed and stared at the floor. There was a rumbling, a low thrumming shake from deep inside the plant. She could feel it through the soles of her shoes: the mixing had started. The newest line of vinyl was at last in production, the phalates bonding with the polymer crystals, mixing, stirring, bonding. She was surprised by how much this part of the building, so far from the heart of the thing, shook and quivered.

IT BEGAN BECAUSE SIMON wouldn't stop asking her questions about where she had left a black towel. The towel was important, indeed it was definitive, though it was only a small hand towel, because something about Amanda had rubbed off on it. She was sweating with nervousness and shame, as though sitting in a math exam, trying to answer questions she couldn't understand.

Simon had told her to go look for the towel herself. That was why she had been on her hands and knees beneath the table. Then she had sunk deeper still and gone underwater. It was whispery green and quiet, and she could feel her hair rising around her head in fat strands. There wasn't a lot of water, just enough to do a small somersault, then there was still less, only enough for Amanda to lie submerged on her back. *Oh, no,* she thought, *I'll come up and everyone will see that I'm naked.* Then she found that she had come up and was sprawled across the tabletop. Simon was staring with disgust at her ankles. Amanda reached out her arm, heavy with water and flesh, to touch her ankle bone, and instead felt the tentacles of a sea anemone, its body growing out of her bone. *Blood star,* she thought. And when she said this, she meant it was filled with her blood and had changed colour because of this. She turned her head to look down and saw that there were actually two anemones, engorged and surprised, growing from the bone of each ankle.

The alarm was screaming, clanging, vituperative. It rang as if to say sleep was a sin. Now it was off. Amanda stared at the ceiling, which had a coffee-coloured stain in its centre. Caused by what? Rain possibly, or an accumulation of water in the bathroom upstairs. An old flood. She could feel the presence of the other tenants in the building, some already up, some still sleeping. In another minute she would have to get up, wash, deodorize, dress—all the rituals that cleansed her of her slightly spicy morning smell.

It was the thought of washing that made her remember her dream.

Ten o'clock.

Simon opened the bathroom door and found Amanda sitting on the edge of the tub, her feet in the water. She smiled at him, abashed at his surprise. She seemed even softer than usual, as though the downy edges of her skin had blurred.

"Amanda," he said. "Amanda, Amanda. What are you doing at home? Are you sick?"

"I think maybe a little."

"Poor sweetie." He sat down on the toilet and stroked the wet tendrils at the back of her neck. "Poor beautiful."

"Oh, Simon."

"It's probably stress from the wedding preparations." He leaned over and kissed her right temple. He put his face closer, rubbed her cheek with his nose. Then he recoiled. "What did you put in the water?"

"Salt," she answered. "And bleach."

"Your feet needed a really good scrub?"

"I don't know. I have a feeling . . . it's hard to explain."

"Try."

She took a deep breath. "I have a feeling," she said. "A feeling . . ." She stopped. "I'm sorry," she said. "It's too hard to explain."

But with his prodding, his delicate care, she managed to tell him about her dream.

"I can't get it out of my head," she said. "I feel as though these things are still there. Growing on me. On my ankles."

"All right then. Let me see."

She lifted her foot. He dried it on the black towel, then touched her ankle, prodding the red bone.

"Here?"

She nodded.

"And here?"

She nodded again.

He looked hard, turning the ankle, stroking the skin. At last he placed her foot back down in the tub.

"I think you're going to be all right," he said. "It's a common or garden ankle, though very clean."

After Simon left, Amanda looked at her right ankle in the water, then her left. It was not that she thought anything was on them; she could see they were clean and bare. It was more what amputees feel when they lose a leg or an arm: the ghost of a limb, still there. Her legs seemed very long, like the pilings under docks, and she felt the tentacles of the sea anemones—*blood stars*—suctioned to her ankle bones. Amanda reached under the toilet for the bottle of bleach. She poured in a splash, then another splash. There was only a bit left in the bottle, so she turned it upside down and emptied it into the tub.

It was ten after eleven and she was very late, sitting in her red Dodge Colt in the parking lot. At the edge of the parking lot was a chain-link fence. On the other side was yellow grass, dry and trembling in the December wind. Beyond the field Amanda felt rather than saw the elephantine curve of Lake Ontario.

Purlex was situated on the Great Lakes so that (though Public Relations denied it) at night they could fling open the pipes and let the effluent pour out from the holds. Sometimes foam rolled up on the nearby beaches. And sometimes, as though part of an abreaction, there were protesters in the parking lot. They always looked ineffectual, Amanda thought, with their hand-painted signs saying things like PVC = CANCER—a little mass of them huddled near the doorway, dwarfed by the building behind them.

She sat back and closed her eyes. It seemed to her that the blood stars had been there a long time, though she had only dreamt of them that morning; that they had been gathering force every time she brushed her teeth, every time she cleansed away her hair with Neet; and that it was her fate, her sullen, private fate, to be infested. Hadn't she always known she was different? Different from whom? Different from everybody—different from Simon, different from Myra.

When she was six, her mother had put her in a red velvet dress with a detachable lace collar and taken her to a photographer. The picture is still on her mother's mantelpiece, among the silver dishes of potpourri, the porcelain salt and pepper shakers shaped like dancing pigs. Whenever Amanda saw that picture, she remembered what she had been thinking as it was snapped: *I must pretend to be myself.* She had put on an expression, a certain look she was supposed to have, and tilted her head like the spaniel in her Grade One reader.

She had always been hiding who she was. The silk blouse, the trim poly-blend pants, didn't really belong to her; they belonged to someone who was pretending to be her, who had picked out these clothes because they were exactly the kind of thing Amanda Melanchuk would wear.

Mr. Kyle smelled of oil this morning, what you would smell if you opened a can of sardines, peeling back the tin tongue with its gold key to see the embarrassing lines of fish covered with hair. Amanda was alone with him in his office.

"If there's nothing else, Mr. Kyle . . ."

"Amanda." He mouthed the word like bread, touching the syllables, feeling them with his tongue. "You know I

want you to help me in the inventory room. There's a new
shipment of crystals that needs to be tallied. I'll show you
the plant on the way. You've never seen the whole thing,
have you?"

"I can't."

"No? Why not?"

"I mean I could, but perhaps one of the other girls
could instead."

"I asked you, Amanda."

"All right then, Mr. Kyle." She tried to sound profes-
sional. "All right then."

In the main office the women watched with smug
faces as Mr. Kyle held open the heavy door that led into
the main body of the plant. On the office side it was oak,
but on the other, the plant side, it was liver-coloured metal.

The hallway walls were yellow, and the air thudded
through lung-like vents above their heads. They walked
awkwardly, purposefully, down the long hallway, then into
a room like a lumber storage room but filled with plastic
strips cut to size, ready to be bundled. Beyond this area the
hallway grew thinner. They came to the mixing room, its
window steamed over like a bathhouse, and Mr. Kyle
rubbed the glass and they looked inside. Amanda caught a
glimpse of men like ghosts in the steam—engineers,

chemists, manual labourers. They were dressed in white protective gear, surgical masks over their mouths. Amanda and Mr. Kyle continued through the filter room, which was filled with pipes and wheels like the engine room of a ship. Grey-bellied tanks murmured, letting out steam, crying like faraway whales. This was where the plasticizing process began, Mr. Kyle yelled to her against the sound. On her wrists and ankles, knees and fingers, she felt the anemones responding, opening their tentacles, searching for food.

Amanda and Mr. Kyle rounded a corner, closed a door, opened another and found themselves in a deserted hallway. He turned toward her, flicked out a hand and grasped her wrist. A charge surged up her arm. His eyes were cold as the cutting edge of a knife.

"I know you. I *watch* you," he said.

She tried to pull her hand loose.

"I watch you," he repeated. "I know what you're like." His tongue made a serpentine visitation to his red upper lip, wetting it.

"Please, Mr. Kyle," she said. She closed her eyes and leaned against the wall. She could feel the balloon of loneliness in him as he leaned close to her. The whispered sigh of his breath. *Things you see and things you don't.* He was telling her that he heard her name in his ear when he drove. And when he lay in bed he felt her body. What was it like? It was like the heat of the sun.

She felt tears spring from the sides of her eyes. Her legs were coated in them, on every crag and surface, even the soles of her feet. But through their pressing flesh she felt the breath of Mr. Kyle, leaning closer, a man born in the mud. She saw this about him, and that wasn't all she saw: she saw his house, his wife, a dormouse with colourless hair, a short dirty sweater, a tired face.

Mr. Kyle bent near her, whispering. "I see your hair in my sleep. I feel you constantly. I go where I think I'll see you."

"Please," she said. "I have to go back."

At last he seemed to notice that she was leaning against the wall, breathing raspily, her skin almost green.

"You're sick," he said. "Stop. Wait. Here—" He held on to her and back they went, through the labyrinth of yellow walls, away from the dull thrumming at the centre of the plant, back toward the kidney-coloured metal door. Mr. Kyle pushed it open. On the other side the girls looked up, smirking. Amanda in the arms of Mr. Gerald Kyle—this was too good to be true.

"She's sick," Mr. Kyle shouted. "Get a chair."

But Amanda had already sunk onto the carpet. She leaned against the wall, eyes closed, holding on to her ankles.

One of the anemones was open on her leg. It was a frowzy pink and orange, bleary at its edges as though from too many washings. It clung to her right calf, fastened to the fat-and-muscle bulge, firmly holding on like a child who won't let go unless its fingers are peeled back one by one. It wasn't real; it was the after-effect of a dream. But this fact only marginally reassured her. In reality she was up to her waist in water. Up to her waist with the tide coming in.

Myra knelt beside her. Myra, who drew in light like black cloth in the desert.

"Are you all right? You're white as a sheet."

"I'm fine. I just need to stand up."

For a moment it occurred to Amanda that her body was stuck to the carpet; but in fact she rose quite easily, with all eyes on her, and began to limp with a faint suctioning slurp and flop toward the door. Her legs were covered—a mass of sea flesh—and she was diminished within herself, almost fainting from their weight and soft boring. She stumbled against Myra, who held out a hand to steady her, and when she did, a spark of static leapt between them. Myra pulled back, shocked, holding out her charged hand.

Her hand was fine, but Amanda was staring at her now with bright, woeful eyes.

"*Eloj,*" Amanda said.

"What did you say—? Where did you hear that? I didn't say that—"

"I heard you say it."

"I didn't say anything." Myra's face was white.

Amanda felt a flood of apprehension, a mist around her eyes, a glint of white and silver dots. There was a slow somersaulting of water deep inside her. She took a step forward and heard Myra's voice, then felt her hand, strong as a claw, gripping her arm.

"I think you should keep the baby," Amanda said, then fell forward in a faint.

Myra took her home, gave her to Simon, who put her to bed.

Amanda slept fitfully and dreamed that Gerald Kyle was laughing down at her, about to extract one of her molars, which had something damaged at its root. When she woke, she found an anemone wedged behind her ear.

Later still she looked up and saw herself in the gilt mirror. White skin. Dark holes for eyes. Body suckered end to end by bright, questioning visitants. They were everywhere: inside her ears, between her fingers, under her arms, in the folds of her vagina. One was pressed against her cervix like a plug. They were squeezed against the fat pulp of each other's bodies, a mass of multiflorous, breathing, sucking flesh.

"I'm dying," she thought. "I'm dying."

For the rest of that day she lay in bed, her body covered with a sheet. Simon called the doctor, who came and knelt beside her. "You have a fever," he said. "That's all. A little fever." He gave Simon instructions to wipe the inside of her elbows with rubbing alcohol every two hours, to bring her temperature down. When he did this, the anemones quivered and shrank. She hoped the solution would cleanse them away.

"I'm sorry," she said to Simon.

"Shh," he said. "Don't be silly. There's nothing to be sorry about."

But the things made her abject and shamed.

She saw. She heard. She lay in bed. Myra came into the room and crept close. "I wanted to see how you were," she said. "Don't worry about me," she added. "I was glad to get the rest of the day off work."

Amanda looked toward the window and saw that it was night now.

"What a great guy your Simon is," Myra said. "Why didn't you ever tell me you were getting married? I love your gown. By the way, you were right." She whispered this last thing fiercely, her face close. "I went to the clinic and they told me right away." She leaned still closer. "Do you see anything else—about my future?"

In the dark Amanda saw a fire between Myra's eyebrows, but she said nothing. Down below she could see the thing like a snail, a coiled baby snake, curled in Myra's belly.

"Oh, don't worry about it," Myra said lightly. "I was just wondering."

Amanda lay stretched out, covered by the sheet. Underneath, the sea creatures moved their tendrils in the cool, dark air. It was a deep source of grief to feel them. But in this lowered place, her ears and eyes were clear, terribly clear. She saw Joe Dunn below, three storeys down, and her mind flooded with images: Little girl. Tartan skirt. She saw a man's face like a bull, felt the pounding of the board on his daughter's ear, the flare of blood, the pain, and then the bruise growing within.

DAY THREE

SHE SAW A RAVEN carrying a starfish in its mouth, its leg almost severed by the beak. It grows back, she told herself, watching from her place on the ground.

Then a lion came. *You're not to tell,* it said, its dark face close to her own, its breath sour with blood and grass. She knew what it meant: not to tell about the space within her, dark and warm, full of liquid honey.

She had dreams all night. They piled on, until she felt she had jogged through them, been lashed or pelted by them.

She woke, her body shaken. Simon was looking down at her.

"How did you sleep?"

"All right."

"I have tea here."

"Thank you."

"Do you need help sitting up?"

"I think I'm all right."

She sat up and he handed her the tea.

"I've been pushing you too hard," he said. "I've been wanting too much. I'm sorry. I'll change if you want me to." He looked at her. "Do you want me to?"

She looked around the room, then back at him. All the

cast-off junk he collected was a yeasty detritus attached to a single blue core in him.

"There's something there," she said, and reached out to touch his chest. They both looked down at what she was reaching for. He felt a shock in his body, which he would never forget, as he half expected her hand to slip inside.

The shape of this place is like a map, but one you follow with your nose, with your hands, through the bulrushes, past the chain-link fence, the brick suburbs. The body of the lake always holds you, due south, a smell that, if you wanted, you could also smell on the palms of your hands.

The white facade of Purlex is a gleaming excrescence, a brilliant, outlandish boil rising from the bog grass and bulrushes. And all around, all around the parking lot, the wind is hissing, a wind similar to that which criss-crossed the marsh a hundred thousand years ago, that blew over the ice in the ice age. Now it tumbles a plastic bag across the parking lot, catches it on the fence, fills and empties it with air.

Ten o'clock.

The artificial leaves of the palm swayed, ever so slightly, to the rumble deepening from the centre of the plant.

"There's something I need from the stockroom," Amanda said to Mr. Gerald Kyle. She stood in front of him, in his office.

"What kind of thing, Amanda?"

"More printout paper," she heard herself whisper. She put out her fingers and touched the edge of his desk.

He looked down her body, then up her body. "Do you think that's wise?" he said. "What about those fumes?"

She held his eyes and did not let go until he pushed back his chair and stood up. Together they crossed the plush carpet of the main office.

"We're going to check the inventory," Amanda said calmly and steadily to Myra as she passed. The girls watched, hushed by what they saw, as Mr. Kyle opened the door leading into the plant. The smell of polymers rose to greet them.

Amanda and Mr. Kyle walked down corridors, into back rooms, pipe rooms, boiler rooms, the air full of steamy fumes that made Amanda thirsty. She took Mr. Kyle by the elbow and led him now, through rooms the size of closets, past metal shelves holding cans of ethylene and phalates, every one of them stamped with the symbol of a corroded hand. She led him down a dark hallway to a storage-room door. Chlorine and Phalate Depository, it said.

She opened the door and let it clank shut behind him.

For a moment everything was blackness. Then the room burst into light as Mr. Kyle pulled a light-bulb chain above his head. The place was filled with bags of laminated burlap. Some of the sacks had tumbled over, strewing chlorine and polymer crystals across the cement floor. Some were blue and white, like laundry detergent, others milky red, and others green.

He backed her up against a bag of crystals.

"Mr. Kyle," she whispered. "Mr. Kyle. I'm covered— with sea things." She held out her wrist, to show him the bone, and quick as an eel he drew it to his mouth, kissed the wrist bone.

He pushed her back onto the bag of crystals. It toppled over and she fell down. She tried to get up, but he grabbed both of her ankles with his hands.

"Do you have them here?" he said.

"I'm covered with them."

"End to end?"

"Like a rock at low tide."

"Let me see—"

"There's one here, at the nape of—"

Kneeling astride her, he undid the buttons of her shirt.

81

"Each one—"

"Lie back—"

She lay back.

"Here?"

She nodded.

"Here?"

He traced the line of her bra, then undid the catch. Nipples. Underarm. Belly button. Each anemone contracted at his touch. Salt tongue in the groove. Let them open. Let them flower.

"Here?" He probed, salt-tongued.

He dug his face into her skirt, into the crotch of her nylon stockings. He pulled them down and nosed her. Inside, an anemone moved its green feathered fingers. A quake shuddered through both of them.

"Is it opening or closing?"

Opening or closing?

"We had better leave separately," Mr. Kyle said, doing up his pants. "I'll go first, you come ten minutes after."

She lay on the floor and watched him tuck his white shirt into his belt. An oily man with vinyl loafers. He licked his fleshy lips, which were red now, like petals. The room stank of the formaldehyde used to kill mice before dissection. Or did this smell come from Mr. Kyle himself—the post-coital reek of a very strange man?

He let himself out of the room. Amanda remained stretched out on the floor. She could still hear his voice close to her ear: *sea pony... sea lion... sea witch*. Had he really said those things? Surely not. But then again, perhaps. He had licked his tongue deep into her, touching the centre of the deepest sea flower, and she had felt it murmur, contract, then open more fully to his touch.

As for the blood stars themselves, they seemed to have fallen asleep.

They had arranged their tendrils within their bodies and drawn themselves closed; though they still covered her end to end, from her ankles to the line of her brow, which they studded like dots of kohl, one between her eyebrows like the mark women of India wear at marriage.

The air in the room felt suddenly clear and cool. Like night air. Dark as velvet. Why me? she thought. But it came to her that this was the best part, that it should happen to herself alone. Only herself. She lay on her back among the spilt granules. The crystals had attached themselves to the flesh of the blood stars, so that every part of her—the crevice of her neck, the cracks between her fingers and toes—was encrusted like an Indian dagger with amber resin, milky rubies, sapphires and peridots and blood-black amethysts. She was utterly magnificent, living and dead, and there was no saying where she left off and the other things began.

sea lions

THE SUN HAD RISEN for several hours above the cedar-covered mountains, the logging scars and the highway, and it shone down now from close to the centre of the sky. It stunted the shadows of two men, one young, one old, walking across the sand of Schooner Bay. They had checked out of their hotel room and had an hour to kill before they were due to arrive at Cedar Point, a retirement home two miles north. The younger man planned to settle his father in and talk to the staff. Then he would begin the long drive across Vancouver Island, back to the city.

They stood in the middle of the beach where the sand was firm and looked towards the black rocks in the bay, near the horizon. Flares of white spray hurtled towards the sky. Sailors had broken their boats on the rocks and died out there, but between the rocks and the shore, the bay itself was remarkably calm. Small waves rolled regularly up the sandy beach, deposited lines of foam, then drew back. Strands of kelp were coiled on the sand like women's hair.

The older man, Thomas, bent down with some difficulty to pick up a stick. It was clean and silvery. He held it in front of him, pointing to an outcropping of rocks at the end of the beach.

"That's where I want to go," he said. "There and back."

It was where they always went on this walk, but Ian, the younger man, shook his head. "We can't get there and back in an hour," he said.

"Then we'll have to take longer."

They began to walk. Every second step Thomas swung his stick forward and planted a small, neat hole in the sand. At one point he stopped, lifted his head like an old dog, and listened to the ragged bawling of a chainsaw that had begun in the hills to the east. Ian stopped too, striking the same pose as his father, head up, listening. Far down the beach the voices of children were picked up, carried by the wind, then lost. Above them a seagull hung in a current of air, scarcely moving.

"Look," Thomas said. He pointed with his stick towards the sea, towards the rocks. On the farthest outcropping he saw hazy forms in the spray. "Sea lions," he said.

Ian peered at the rocks. "I'm not so sure," he said. "I don't think we get sea lions this time of year."

His father pointed again. "There—on the northwest corner of that rock."

Ian shaded his eyes and peered into the bay. "That's discoloration on the rock face," he said at last.

"No. Not there. *There.*" Again his father pointed with the stick.

"I don't see anything."

"You're not looking in the right place."

Ian shrugged.

His father turned to him, exasperation on his face. "You should learn how to examine things," he said. "Learn to see. It's the first law of empiricism. You can't be a good doctor if you don't know how to look at things."

"I know how to look at things."

"But not hard enough."

"I know how to look hard enough. Anyway, we'll see when we reach the telescope."

"*You'll* see."

They walked more quickly. Above the high-water mark, by the tangle of bramble bushes, two men with dreadlocks squatted beside an orange pup tent, cooking. A naked woman knelt beside them. All at once she stood up and ran down the beach towards the water, passing Ian and Thomas. She ran across the wet sand, coils of dark hair bouncing on her back, then galloped into the surf, lifting her knees high, plunging headfirst into a wave. She stood up and faced them, gleaming in the sun, waving her arms.

Thomas lifted his stick and waved back.

"She's not waving at us," Ian said. "Look over there."

Behind them, the two men had stripped off their jeans and stood naked, their penises white against their black pubic hair. They waved back at the woman, then ran down the beach towards her. One called out something as he passed.

"What did he say?" Thomas asked.

"He said, 'Better luck next time.'"

"Why? Why did he say that?"

"Because you waved at her."

They continued their walk along the beach. "Better luck next time," Thomas repeated. "Better luck next time. That's what I need: better luck."

Ian gave his father a look, as though to say, *Do you really want to get into all that?*

"What?" said his father. "I'm just saying I could use better luck." He took a handkerchief from his trousers' pocket, wiped his upper lip and forehead, then folded it slowly and pushed it back into his pocket. "*You're* the one," he continued, "who said I couldn't see what was right in front of my own eyes."

"I didn't say that."

"You implied it."

"I simply couldn't see the sea lions myself."

"I could. But what difference does that make? If I press my point, you'll say I'm imagining things. The old man's mind is wandering, you'll say."

"No, I won't."

"Well, maybe I'm imagining that too, eh?"

Ian and Thomas walked on in silence.

"They shouldn't be swimming naked on a public beach," Ian said.

"At least that's one thing we agree on."

They didn't talk for a long while. The sky was clear and blue above them, the surf crashed and crashed against the distant rocks, and all around it smelled of rotting seaweed. It was a good smell, a smell of things that had stayed in the sea a long time before getting tossed onto the shore. Looked at objectively, it was a good day, nothing wrong with it. Bolstered by this thought, Ian turned to his father and said gently, "Listen: I know this isn't exactly what you expected. But it's a good place. And I really think that, with time, you'll adjust."

"I'll adjust, will I?" Thomas kept his head down, watching his stick poke holes evenly, every two feet, in the sand.

"We always thought Mother would be there, and that somehow she would take care of things. But she's not."

Thomas kept watching the holes his stick was making, then all of a sudden he raised it and slapped at a seagull. "Get away. Git," he called.

"And you can go for walks every day, walks on this beautiful beach."

"With a nurse escorting me. And a bunch of old invalids."

"You heard the man: the nurse is simply there in case someone falls down—"

"Or wanders off, or drowns."

"You'll be just like you were in the big house. Nothing will be all that different. You'll have your newspaper. Your tea. The only difference is that a group of competent people will be looking after you."

"I don't need people looking after me."

"You think you don't, but you do. You fell down the stairs and almost broke your hip."

"I slipped because of that damned woman. She washed the steps and didn't tell me."

"For whatever reason. You can't live alone any more. It's not safe. I know you know that."

Thomas seemed to be thinking about this point,

possibly recognizing the necessity and the logic of what his son had said. But when he spoke again, it was clear that this wasn't the case. "I told you when you married her," he said. "I told you that a woman who runs her own practice wouldn't have time for other things. Like children."

"That's our business."

"Well, it's my business now, isn't it? It's my business if I'm left here, because Kate doesn't want to have people around."

"To be fair, Father, it's not just Kate. It's the entire situation. You know it would never work for you and me to live together."

"Why not?"

"Oh, Father. You know all the reasons. Look at us. I've never been able to say anything that was right. Even the sea lions: I say I can't see them, and you use it as an excuse to lecture me about empiricism."

"I've worked all my life to teach you the things I value."

"You used to drill me. I remember once I hid under Mother's sewing table just so you wouldn't make me recite the chemical elements."

The old man stopped. "I wouldn't make you say the elements now," he said, and his son laughed, and put an arm around his father's shoulders.

91

"Father," he shook his head, "it's just not possible."

Thomas pushed the arm away, and started to walk again.

They were very close to the outcropping of black rocks at the end of the beach. There was a flat area on one of them to which the metal stand of the telescope had been riveted. The beach had thinned, the forest was close now, and a breeze from beyond the point chilled the sweat on their cheeks. The grinding of the chainsaw grew to a scream, then cut away in silence. They heard the cracking of a tree trunk before it hit the ground.

"It's because of your mother," the older man said. "That's why, isn't it?"

Ian shook his head.

"I provided for her for forty-two years, don't you forget that." Thomas thrust his stick into the sand. "The day she died was the saddest in my life. And don't think I don't miss that woman."

"Let's not get into that."

"On her deathbed I apologized for everything I did. She took me in her arms and she said she forgave me. That's what she said."

"She would say that."

"That's just my point. She and I understood each

other, don't think we didn't. She knew I never wanted to hurt her."

"I don't want to talk about it."

"Now what would she think, seeing me like this? She never would have wanted this, Ian."

Ian wheeled around. "Don't you tell me what Mother would have wanted," he said. "Don't you dare do that. You don't have the right."

They stood in the shadow of the rock, Ian staring at his father, Thomas wheezing heavily. Then Ian started to walk again. "Now let's go and look through the telescope," he said. "We're late."

They climbed slowly up the slanted rock face, holding on to crannies. Ian offered his father his hand, but Thomas shook his head and crawled up by himself, on his hands and knees, then stood up slowly and clutched the bronze telescope. Down below, the water was green and hectically churning. A seagull dropped a mussel onto the rocks and it broke open.

Thomas propped his hands on his knees, bent down and peered through the telescope towards the rocks. At first he saw only indistinct green and white flecks, but as he squinted he saw, on the farthest rocks, the bodies of sea lions, round and opulent, like fat women sunning themselves. Fountains of foaming water cascaded around them.

He said something that Ian couldn't hear.

"What?" Ian said. "What did you say?"

"If you could forgive me," his father said, "if you could do that, we could go down to that water and get a drink."

"You're tired—"

"I'm not tired, I tell you. I just know how things are. I want you to forgive me." He reached out and grasped his son by the hand, squeezing the soft skin at the base of his thumb.

Ian shook his head. "There's nothing to forgive," he said. "You're tired, that's all."

He pried his father's fingers away and led him to a mound in the rock. Thomas sat down while Ian went and looked through the telescope at the blue sky and the black rocks. By the time he came back, his father was himself again. He breathed hard and then pulled himself up.

"It was too far to come," Ian said. "I knew that."

His father said nothing. He held his son's arm and they stepped carefully down the sloped surface of the rock. They walked back along the beach, side by side, until at last Ian thought of something he could say to break the silence.

"I wish there *had* been sea lions out there," he said. "I really do."

the falling woman

SOME OF MY DREAMS feel like memories. In one, Mother has cornered me in a stall. She is trying to get me to close my teeth over the snaffle bit. But it's massive in my mouth, it tastes like tin and the green spit of horses, if it is pushed over my tongue I will gag. Her hands are as fierce as weasels' claws, and they are tugging at the sides of my mouth.

In another I am bareback on Douna, her quarter horse, while Mother is below and behind me. I can see the shadow of her black hat. The dry hills rise around us, pulsing with crickets. Then Mother slaps Douna's rump and yells *grip*, but I can't grip, I can only bounce on my crotch in the white sunlight, watching the dirt blur while I tip away and fall.

Once, Ben and I were lying here staring at the dark ceiling, and he asked me about my childhood. I grew up in the Okanagan Valley. It was dry, I said. There were cactuses about the size of your thumb bunched around the grey rocks. Hidden punishments. Tell me about your mother, he said. I changed the subject.

I don't talk about her. I dream her. As I walk along

the slushy street, or heat my plastic dish of Stouffer's Veal Parmigiana in the microwave, I see the hills rising up, leached of colour, speckled by pines. Sauble Mountain curves above the flats like a reclining hip, a granite cliff cut into it, revealing the etched outline of a falling woman. It is hard to see her, it always was; you have to focus or have someone else point her out, and even then she is partly wishful. Her hair is five milky fissures. Her arching body is a scar in the rock, like a pock on the moon's face. She fled a marriage her father had arranged—according to an Okanagan legend—galloping in the dark up the back of the mountain. But as she reached the top, the moon disappeared; she lost her way and plunged off the cliff.

I see Mother's legs, bowed from riding, her jeans tucked into her steel-toed boots, her checkered shirt that must have belonged to my grandfather—*Papa*. I see her belt with the cattle horns engraved on the buckle; they meet in the middle like a crescent moon. I see Mother's arthritic knuckles, her thumbs strong as crowbars. She rolls up her sleeve and throws down her hand, thumb up, on the kitchen table, daring Uncle Nesbit to a thumb wrestle. I see her walking out into the dirt yard, the screen door slapping behind her. She walks low in her hips because they ache, still, from my uncompromising birth—the only thing that was bigger than she was, the only thing that knocked her sideways, got her thumb down and twisted until she screamed.

All day today I couldn't picture her face; it blurred under her hat brim. Then I closed my eyes to sleep and her stare burned into me, her mouth curled. I could see her gold incisor, the yellowed skin of her throat. *Ellen,* she screamed, and I sat up in bed. *What the hell do you think you're doing?* Nothing, I wanted to say. I wanted to hold out my hands, show I hadn't touched myself. Then I remembered—she's dead. Any voices I hear come from me.

But now I can't fall back to sleep. I'll pay for it tomorrow. I'll be light-headed as I clean teeth with my little tools—the tiny scaler, the suction hose, the miniature bowls that hold the prophy gel. This kind of work is like playing Barbie: everything's tiny, even the teeth reflected in the mirror.

Today I picked out parsley from behind a patient's molar, then I poked my head into Dr. Stephen French's office. He had X-rays of an impacted wisdom tooth spread on his desk, the photograph of his wife and twin sons on the wall behind him. He looked up, startled, his eyes rimmed by round glasses, like dark birds caught in a trap. Then he followed me down the hall and we studied the

patient together, under the heated lamp. When I passed Dr.
French the silver amalgam, I saw a mole near his collar.

One of these days I may close his office door behind
me. *Look at this strange occlusion,* he will say, and I will stand
behind him, observing the ghostly markings of teeth. Then
I will touch that mole with my finger. He will close his
eyes and shudder like a horse.

I never knew my father. When I was six, Selena, my cousin
from Vancouver, told me I had been born out of wedlock
with a hired man. I had seen Mother demonstrate a headlock on Walt, our current hired man. He'd stood stock-still
like a rabbit and remonstrated softly, *Now really, Mary,*
before landing on his back on the floor. When Selena
mocked me that day, I knew Mother must have done
something unseemly, like the headlock on Walt, that had
made my father want to disappear.

It was only when I was twelve that I got the facts from
Aunt Clara, Selena's mother. That was the summer they
drove into the dirt turnaround in a red convertible—
chrome fenders, spokes and white vinyl top all shining at
once. Selena sat proudly in the front, dressed in red-and-
white seersucker, and when she stepped out carefully, so as
not to dirty the white leather on her saddle shoes, I saw

that her dress had a magnificent bow at the back. I instantly wanted it. I wanted everything Selena had with a complete, black need the minute I saw it.

That night after supper I had Aunt Clara to myself. Selena had begged off the dishes, saying she was sick—but I knew she was soaking in the bathwater reading the Signet Romance she'd shown to me, furtively, that afternoon. Mother had gone to check on Douna's foal. As her lantern disappeared into the barn, Clara sighed. A shudder of regret seemed to pass over her, exhaled from her pores along with the smell of gin. Her hair was stiff with spray. She wore a blue angora sweater, with a necklace of round, pink stones. They looked like beads of flesh. I could tell by the pointy shape of her breasts that she had on one of her marvellous brassieres. Florets, mesh, underwire, clasps: the armour of femininity.

I knew why she sighed. Seeing Mother disappear into the barn had reminded Clara of her own place in the world, on the ranch. After Mumma died Clara had been given the role of the feminine sister, the stay-inside-the-house sister, the one who did all the cooking. She had told me all the stories: How Papa and my mother were inseparable. How, when she was only three, Papa had given her a gelding named Gibraltar. How Mother used to follow

Papa out to the barn, sit next to him as he milked the cows, while he recited poems to her—the *Rubáiyát of Omar Khayyám* or verses from Coleridge. *A damsel with a dulcimer in a vision once I saw . . .* For some reason it hurt to hear these stories.

"What was my father like?" I asked.

Aunt Clara scrubbed at a casserole dish, her forearms swaying. He had a thin face and dark hair, she said, and he could blow smoke rings just by snapping his jaw. He sounded like the men at Dan's, the main bar in Keremeos. As we hurried by the half-open door one afternoon, my mother's boots clumping on the boardwalk, I had glimpsed men in the darkness, one leaning back in his chair, his T-shirt hitched above his white stomach. He was digging at his belly button as we passed, fishing out lint. I could also see the eyes of other men, glinting near the pool table, hear the smack of pool balls. I couldn't picture my mother succumbing to any man, but her particular disgust at the men who visited Dan's—the way she gripped my hand, then yanked it as laughter rolled out of the darkness (at us? I couldn't tell)—made it all that much harder to imagine.

"I think she did it to rebel against Papa," Clara said, scouring at the glass casserole beneath the filmy water. "But it backfired. When Papa found out, he swore he'd horse-whip Les if he didn't marry her—and horsewhip your mother if she didn't agree."

Clara stopped and looked out toward the barn. We could see Mother's light through the feed-room window.

"Then Papa had his stroke, out in the field. After he was buried, your mother told Les to get going. Get going or she'd run him off."

"But why?"

"That's your mother." Clara shook her head. "I guess she couldn't stand the thought of having him around one more second." She pulled out the plug and let the brownish water drain away.

After Mother died, I found an old picture of her at the bottom of the horse-medicine cupboard. She is about fourteen, standing on the back of Gibraltar, holding the reins like a circus performer, smiling brazenly into the camera. I could see the defiant beginning of anger—of wanting to be a boy, being told she should have been a boy, and being wrapped in a girl's body. I imagine her crossing the bare yard to the horse barn in the afternoon sun, her shadow elongated in the dirt. She flattens her new breasts with her forearms so she will not see them in her shadow. She is fiercely repelled by the growth of her body—for good reason. It will prove fertile as a chicken's egg. It will betray her.

My feet ache from a day squeezed in high-heeled slip-ons. I wouldn't be caught dead in orthopaedics. That would be the beginning of the end, the spiral toward old age, which starts with orthopaedic shoes, moves to opaque stockings, then spreads up to swallow hips, back and finally hair. The last stage is when the scalp shows beneath the dyed strands of henna. Then it's death; the body lies back and comes apart, only the bones and teeth left, gleaming against the soil.

It was two months ago this weekend that Ben and I drove to his sister's cottage on Lake Huron. We arrived at night and made love in darkness. As I tried to sleep, tossing in the strange bed, the wind threw sand at the kitchen window. Next morning I saw that the whitewashed shingles had blown away in chunks, leaving gaps of tarpaper.

I walked to the beach and let the wind hit me. When I came back, I found Ben around the side, out of the wind, chopping driftwood into splinters. He held on to the wood for too long, then brought the axe down and almost nipped off his fingers.

"I need to talk to you," he said.

We squatted next to the house, looking out at the garden of driftwood, listening to the wind moaning against the boards.

"I've been in agony." The words came out with his hot breath. "I've decided to tell Judy. Maybe she'll take me back, maybe she won't, but I have to come clean."

On the drive home I sat beside him, not saying a word, drinking coffee from my Styrofoam cup, drawing lines in it with my thumbnail. Ben had taken a shower before we left and his hair was wet; even his nose shone. "I have a lot to thank you for," he said. I peeled away a bit of cuticle and left a pink crescent beside my thumbnail.

Now I yank the blinds down, they rattle to the radiator, and when I turn the plastic wand, there is darkness. Back in bed, I ease my legs out, leaning on one hip, trying to find the position that will let me sleep.

The day after Selena and Aunt Clara arrived at the farm, Selena and I made a plan to go to the stable, to read her paperback together. But in the morning we changed the sprinklers in the horse pasture, then drove with Mother and Clara into town. It was late afternoon before she and I slid the stable door open on its runner, then closed it behind us. Inside, the clay floor retained its coolness. I could hear Douna blowing through her nose. Mother's collection of tack hung on the walls around us—bridles with bits dangling down, reins coiled around each other, western saddles splayed on their racks.

We hoisted ourselves onto the wall between two stalls and sat with our legs dangling down, watching the colt nurse from Douna's swollen teat. Selena took a frosted lipstick from her red purse.

"Put some on," she offered.

"I can't," I said. "My mother will see."

"What's she going to do? Whip you?" She made a shiver of feminine contempt—for my mother for whipping me, for me for being whipped. Then she reached into her purse again, drawing out, at last, the dog-eared paperback: *My Darling Ravager!* On the front a pirate captain, his shirt streaming open at the chest, clenched the hilt of his sword with one hand, while with his other he grasped a woman by the waist. Her back was arched, her lips open and her eyes closed. "Swooning with desire," Selena explained.

She leafed to a place she had marked. "This is the part where the pirate captain has tied Lady Birkwith in the hold. Listen to this: *'You swine,' she cried out, her violet eyes flashing, 'you'll pay for this.' He gave her a mocking half-smile, then she felt his strong arms grip her. She breathed in his murky scent, gasping as his mouth found hers. She tried to struggle but found she could not, did not want to. A hot tide of passion surged through her. Then she gasped again, as the sweet torture of his hands began to unlace the bodice of her gown."*

We looked at each other and laughed.

"How big are your breasts now?" she asked.

"I don't know."

"Mine are bigger than last year," she said. She pulled open the elastic collar of her dress and showed me a cotton training bra. She tossed her Alice in Wonderland blond hair back over her shoulders. "Well, let's see yours."

I untucked my checked shirt from my jeans and lifted it up.

"Ooh," she said, "you've got dark nipples."

I felt a blush of shame course through me. Her hair was blond; mine was a tangle of muddy curls. Her nipples were pink; mine were an unseemly dark shade, like eggplant. I knew my face in the dusk was plain and pinched like my mother's.

I got Papa's bridle from its peg. It was an ancient thing with cross reins and a breast harness for barrel racing. I'd polished it many times, a painful process, particularly in the hot summer: so much leather to rub back and front with saddle soap, so many bits of plated silver.

"You be Lady Birkwith," I said. "I'll tie you in the hold."

She rolled her eyes but agreed, lowering herself reluctantly onto the hay-strewn floor of the empty stall. She held out her hands and I laced the reins around her wrists.

"Ouch, that pinches," she said.

I unhooked the clip of the harness and wrapped it around her forearms, over her breasts. I watched my dark weasel hands knot the leather around the steel base of the manger. We looked at each other and Selena giggled.

"This is so silly," she said.

"I know." The white leather of her saddle shoe glowed where it stuck out in front of her. I pushed back her skirt on her thigh.

"What are you doing?" she giggled.

"Just something." The sun had sunk beneath the high window. I ran my fingers along the straps of her training bra.

"Oh, Pirate," she laughed. "Don't do that."

"I'll do what I like," I sneered. Then I whispered, "The sweet torture of my hands are touching the bodice of your dress." I pushed up her skirt until her white underwear showed. Then I pushed my finger against the cotton crotch.

"Don't," she said suddenly.

"Why not?"

"I don't like it."

"Too bad."

I pulled back the elastic of her underwear at the leg and looked at her vagina, which was bare still, like a child's.

"Untie me," she hissed.

"No."

"You untie me this instant or I'm going to tell Aunt Mary."

"I don't care."

I took a piece of hay and dabbed it in a mound of fresh green manure, then I ran it along the white leather of her shoes, over her frilled ankle socks and up her dress. I smudged it across the pink sateen-covered barrettes and dabbed it on each of her cheeks. She started to cry.

"Be quiet," I said. "They'll hear you." She cried like a child, not caring what noise she made. I shook her a bit, but she started crying harder. "Stop it."

"You let me go," she wailed.

"Stop it, or I'm going to smack you."

She let out another howl and I slapped her across the face. My palm tingled. She abruptly stopped crying and looked at me.

"Please," I whispered. "Stop crying and I'll let you go."

Her mouth turned down and she drew a long gulp of air, then let out another howl.

"I'm going then," I said. I stood up and walked out of the stall. I closed it behind me and leaned against the door. She kept crying.

"I'm going," I called out to her, and this time I did. I slid the stable door closed and walked down the road, across the flats to the base of Sauble Mountain. I climbed up the path until I came to my favourite rock, which had retained heat in the dusk like a warm-blooded animal. I sat on it, looking down at the flats, the barn, the house.

Night came. I heard Mother hollering, our collie Freya barking, then Clara's concerned voice. Two black figures approached the barn and went in. Then, a short while later, they came out. Selena's silhouette blended with her mother's. I waited until the moon came up, large and full, until the rock had grown cold and I was shivering. Then I walked back down. The bunch grass looked cool and very clear, and the stars overhead shone with a painful brilliance.

My heels ground the dirt as I crossed the turnaround. Then I saw a glint of silver near the horse barn, in the shadow of the ponderosa pine. It was Mother, the bit of

Papa's bridle dangling from her hand. I walked across the bright yard toward her, until I was close. She stared at the ground.

"I don't know why I did it," I said. My tears were a dark tar I couldn't release.

She still made no move to punish me. The bridle hung limp in her hand. I had a feeling that if I crossed the moonlit dirt, she would reach out and enfold me, I would breathe the suede of her jacket. Then a breeze bristled the pine, the moon went behind a cloud. "Mother?" I called, because I couldn't see her face.

She was against me. I felt her clench my collar. "You're a bad girl, aren't you?"

"No," I said. "It was Selena—"

"You're a very bad girl." I felt her breath on my face. She yanked me around to face the stable wall. "Say you're bad," she said, pulling up my shirt.

"I'm bad," I cried, as the reins whistled through the air, biting into my back. I clung to the siding as she hit me.

Afterwards, as I lay on my bed in the dark, the door opened. It was Aunt Clara; I could tell from the smell of lemony talcum. She was wearing her Chinese-style dressing gown of turquoise and red satin, which rustled softly as she sat on the side of the bed. She lifted my shirt and looked at the welts, and then she sighed—for me, for Selena, for my mother, perhaps even for Papa, though he was dead. It was a sorrow she felt deeply, and it would carry me for awhile—three days, perhaps four days—until it was time for her to get back into her red-and-white convertible, wave to us and return to the coast.

After a while I felt her touching my hair. At first I thought she was stroking it, but then I realized that she held a small wooden comb.

"People do things they regret," she said.

I didn't answer. And I suppose she didn't expect me to. Instead I lay still, letting her soft hands move over my hair, taking out the tangles.

Mother died of pelvic cancer when I was seventeen. She's buried in the flat expanse of graves near Keremeos. I picked out a slab as marker, nothing else. It says:

> *I've gone to where the darkness ends,*
> *To where the wind blows free,*
> *I've gone away from this small world,*
> *To face my master eternally.*

I don't think she would have liked it, especially the part about the master.

Fourteen floors down, I can hear the thud of cars crossing the steel bridge that draws the four lanes from the QEW into the three lanes of the Gardiner. Beyond is the grey body of the lake, untouchable, serenely polluted. When I close my eyes at last, I travel down the freeway, past the frozen neck of the lake, and I look down on the moonlit farm, the whispering corn flats, the old horse barn. Black and white and grey and dun and roan, the horses wait, blowing through their noses. Mother's teeth gleam where she sits on Douna, under the soughing pine. I swing behind, resting my body against her back, and then we begin to canter toward the top of the mountain.

sugar bush

I HAD COME FROM TORONTO by train, travelling along the rim of Lake Ontario, then turning north, out of the slush, into the snow, into the Ottawa Valley. A place of real cold, real winter. Not the lake-warmed snow of Toronto in February, but the bitter, thirty-below cold of another region entirely.

Carol picked me up at the train station. Tony, her husband, was away for two weeks with an aid team, in Zimbabwe. That's why we had chosen this weekend to be together.

I could describe Carol's dirty blond hair, tied back in a ponytail, the surprising amount of grey in it suddenly (by-product of motherhood); or her long down coat, her mannish winter boots; or the children, I could describe them—Emma in a corduroy baby carrier strapped on Carol's front, Damian, her five-year-old, sitting in the car across the street from the station. ("He didn't want to get out," Carol said, something I took, without wanting to, as an accusation.) I could give an account of boots, coat, hair, children—but why describe them, when what was important, has always been important, were Carol's eyes. Grey

112

eyes of such exceptional clarity. Quaker eyes, I have always thought, because when I first met Carol, ten years ago, she was a Quaker. A lawyer/peace-organizer/Quaker.

"Oh god," she said. "It's good to see you." I had to stand on my toes and reach over the lump that was baby carrier and baby in order to put my arms around Carol. As we hugged, I stared at those grey hairs, close up, while she, no doubt—even in this awkward position—felt my added weight under my navy wool coat. She probably took in, in a flash, how I'd dressed too lightly for the cold; how I'd done this without thinking, because I can never picture the weather in another place until I've travelled into it.

We drove through the village of Dalford, towards Carol's farmhouse. I glimpsed a 7-Eleven, a video arcade and, further out of town, a general store that still, so Carol told me, sold rock candy by the pound. I exclaimed, in my somewhat theatrical way, that the Ottawa Valley was delightful, a walk back in time, though the place actually looked quite dismal. I had expected Victorian gingerbread trim, ample porches, weathercocks on shingled roofs. Instead, farmhouses sat gloomily and stoically in fields of snow, out of which cropped ancient rocks, part of the Canadian Shield, and wild-looking clumps of juniper. The limbs of these bushes grew back, Carol said, no matter how many times they were hacked away.

Every now and then she glanced over at me, but not quite as often as I turned to look at her. I have always been the greedier one, the heavier, the darker. She has the clarity of a piece of bone, and I—well, I have something else. I used to wear Birkenstocks, peacock-feather earrings, used to tie my frizzy hair back in a long braid. Now it's cut short, a curly-locked look that I'm determined to believe is gypsyish. I was wearing Toronto black. Artist's black. I'm an actress now, so I have the getup. My feet were cold in their fashionable but inadequate leather ankle boots.

I planned to tell Carol, as soon as we had a moment, that I had reached the age of the Great Falling Off—how I defined my mid-thirties. Men no longer pierced me with looks of predatory lust as I walked down Queen Street, and this erasure was a surprising source of pain. So now I had five piercings: one in my nose, one in my belly button, three in my right ear, and I wore tight skirts, publicly announcing that I was finally ready to flaunt my sexuality. But too late. Nobody wanted to look at me.

Then I planned to tell her about my botched affair with Derek, a married director. My abysmal, self-effacing last moments with him. How I had opened up, in the end, like an enormous, insatiable clam and attempted to swallow him whole. Then Carol and I would get serious, asking ourselves just exactly why men were so terrified of women. I imagined us sitting in matching rocking chairs beside a fire. She would tell me that all the cracks and fissures in me—crannies teeming with god knows what—were precisely what fascinated her.

"I have things to tell you," I said.

"Do you?" She sounded wistful, vulnerable. "What kind of things?"

"About a man."

She sighed and then said: "I have a story too." She was avoiding my eyes, and I wondered why. Of course it was hard for her to drive, talk *and* look at me. But that wasn't the reason she glanced away. I had the impression that even saying *I have a story too* had cost her something.

Carol heated up some homemade pea soup and we ate lunch in the big kitchen. Her house was like the others in the Valley: built, by Presbyterians no doubt, to withstand the elements. It was shaped exactly like the houses that children draw: red brick, two storeys, with a peaked roof and small, square windows. Old shag carpeting covered the living-room floor—truly depressing—and the faint but persistent odour of rancid margarine seeped from somewhere. Above this smell, like the high note in a perfume, I could detect the acidic reek of pee-soaked diapers. I imagined many of them, possibly hundreds, stewing in the bathroom, in an enormous pail.

As we ate, I told her about Derek. She listened, groaning in the appropriate places. I even described stopping a rehearsal and insisting, in front of the entire cast, that Derek come outside to duke it out. At this Carol stopped buttering her muffin, mid-stroke, and said that I had a remarkable capacity to open myself up.

"Oh sure—to slings and arrows. And abuse." But her appreciation felt like a heat lamp on my chest. My urge to slide inside Derek's skin, the way I had leaked my needs up and down the hallways of the theatre—all this behaviour seemed (with Carol's gentle ministrations) like a kind of bravery. Of course I had a right to demand closeness, she was saying. "But, poor Melanie," she added, "things do seem to go wrong a lot."

I make a mistake with people I admire: I splash in, too fast, then something inside me swells with need. Perhaps this swollen part gives off an offensive odour of desire and deprivation, because, my God, how quickly the other person senses it. And when they withdraw, I want to reach out and grab them by the shirt collar; I want to insert myself inside them.

I glanced at Carol buttering Damian's muffin, looking as though she wasn't fully listening, and I remembered how often I had wanted to get inside her, not just to understand the complexity of her thoughts, but in order, in a sense, to hammer her with my own feelings, to force myself on that tantalizing but unassailable being. When we first met, in the peace movement, she always talked about creating lasting change, how necessary it was, and how, against the societal transformation she had in mind, our petitions, peace pledges and demonstrations were just so much chaff, of no import.

We used to talk about this kind of thing in a bar on Bloor Street. "So be specific," I'd say. "How do you change people?"

She would look into the middle distance, as though declining a complicated Latin noun, then she would smile perplexedly. She believed in an end to violence but could never describe how to begin to make it happen. All she knew was that my tactics weren't sufficient.

Anyway—here she was. The need for deep societal change seemed to have landed her here, in the Ottawa Valley, home-schooling Damian, playing Eve to Tony's Adam.

Her son pulled at her sleeve, said his soup was too hot. She turned to him, the same expression of deep listening on her face as she had used on me, then gravely went to the freezer and got an ice cube. A smudge of motherhood seemed to cover her. A film of distraction. Her breasts were enlarged from feeding Emma. The kitchen floor was cluttered with plastic baby toys and big pieces of Lego. Her chair leg knocked a roly-poly chime ball every time she stood up.

She gave Damian the ice cube (he wanted to put it in his soup himself), then turned to me. "Look at Damian's eyes," she said. "They're the same colour as the slate rocks around Dalford."

I muttered something suitably appreciative, hoping to turn the conversation back to me—but it was too late. Carol was now telling me about Emma's benign and complex character. (She's nine months old, I was tempted to respond, she doesn't *have* a character.) She lovingly described the heart-shaped red birthmark on Emma's rear. When I asked, politely, what could cause something like that, Carol merely shrugged. "It's part of the unknown," she said.

After lunch we sat down together, one at each end of the couch, our feet tucked under a brown-and-orange afghan.

Emma had finally gone down for her nap, and Damian was watching *The Magic School Bus* in the summer kitchen. Through one small window I could see into the field, where a diseased apple tree stood. At the edge of the field there was a split-rail fence with a small gate in it, leading into a sugar bush.

"So tell me what's up," I said. "Something's happened."

Carol bit her fingernail, then looked at me over her hand—a lost, smitten expression on her face.

"You've met someone."

She made a breathy, nervous laugh through her nose, a noise I had never before heard her make. "Met someone," she said. "Yes, you could say that." She looked down at the shag carpeting, the clutter of toys and cloth books and baby paraphernalia. "It's not a normal story. Not something I can explain. Which is why I want to tell you. If I can talk things through with a girlfriend, maybe I'll begin to understand what's happening."

A girlfriend. Not me, Melanie. Just a girlfriend.

"I can't figure any of it out," she said, a tinge of real exasperation in her voice. Sometimes she really did expect problems to yield to logic. When she delivered Damian, she had him at home, in the summer kitchen, squatting between the wall and the stove, pushing and pushing, and finally birthing him before the midwife or Tony arrived. *But it hurt so much,* she said to me on the telephone later, and her tone had been as close as it ever came to petulance, as though she couldn't understand why—when *she* did it all so well—it should still have to be such terrible agony.

—

The story began with a visit to a doctor named Michael Hagopian. Tony knew him from a men's encounter group he had attended: lots of discussions about divorce, problems with custody; lots of drumming. Eventually Tony left, tired of the hostility. But when Carol discovered that Emma was in the full breech position, he suggested Michael Hagopian. He was well known in the Valley for alternative medical treatment, something halfway between the physical and the psychological.

He lived in a small house two miles to the south of theirs, on a parallel road. A stretch of his property, a large tract of maple forest, adjoined their farmland. But his office was in Ottawa, on a nondescript street not far from downtown, in a concrete medical building with glazed, black windows. Carol approached the building, seven months pregnant, stepping carefully over the yellow ice and salt on the sidewalk. Her hips felt loose at the joints, as though her pelvis had expanded and the bones fit sloppily.

She took an elevator to the sixth floor, opened the door marked M. HAGOPIAN, MD, FRCPS—a list of medical credentials that she had to admit she found reassuring. The waiting room too was conventional, with charcoal carpeting and chairs with orange seats and square arms. There were copies of *People*, *Good Housekeeping* and *McCall's* in the magazine rack. And there was a real receptionist, a butch-looking woman with short dark hair and pitying eyes.

"Have you ever been to Michael before?" she asked. When Carol said no, the receptionist gave her arm an alarmingly strong squeeze, as though to test how well-fleshed she was. "You're going to like him," she said. "It's amazing what he can do. But you have to free your mind."

She showed Carol into another, smaller room and told her to take off her clothes, lie down on the leather table and cover herself with the blue flannel sheet. Carol did as she was told.

After several minutes Dr. Hagopian came into the room. He was in his mid-forties, with a hound-like nose and a thin mouth. His cheeks were pitted from an old case of acne, a few small marks the size of rice grains lodged beneath his skin. They weren't disfiguring, especially once you were used to them; they added a background interest to his face. His pupils were dilated, as though he might be taking antidepressants.

Hagopian: it was an Armenian name, Carol found out later.

"So, you're Tony Eccles's wife," he said, defining her, in that Biblical way, by the man who owned her. Daughter of Lot. Wife of Job.

"And you're Michael Hagopian." He was wearing a medical coat over a checked flannel shirt, corduroy trousers. Why the coat? It felt like a disguise. He gave off a noticeable smell, not unpleasant, of wool socks left on a radiator to dry. Carol found out later it was from the mugwort oil he used in herbal acupuncture treatments.

He pulled back the sheet, a quick, brutal gesture, then looked down at her, taking in her breasts lolling to either side, her pregnant stomach, the stretch marks, like a silvery pattern of frost radiating downwards from her belly button. He studied her pubic hair, then looked into her eyes.

"This is called compassionate viewing," he said. "It's the first stage of healing."

His gaze, eyes narrowed, continued to take in her body. If done right, he told her, you could look so deeply into the other person that you could actually absorb their suffering. *If done right,* he said again.

The room was colder than any doctor's office she had ever been in. And her belly felt chilled too. She could feel the baby, foot against her pubic bone, kicking at her.

He was looking at her thighs, looking at her stretch marks. Then he reached out and put his hands on her belly.

"Your baby's in the breech position," he said. But hadn't the nurse simply told him that?

"I know," she said, tight-lipped. Frozen. "That's why I'm here."

But his hands felt good, better than she had imagined they could, in this awful room. The palms of his hands were hot, like rocks in the sun. And his eyes didn't leave hers. Were they hostile or warm? She couldn't tell.

"I want to know what I should do," she whispered. "Can you get the baby to move?"

"It will move on its own, when it's ready. You have to wait. Get in tune with your body. And only do what's right for your baby. Don't think about anything else."

She went back to him three times.

He told her his theories as she lay on the table, under his unfeeling gaze, his warm hands. He talked about what he called women's true natures. Women have the deepest groundwater in them, he said, but they deny it, which causes sickness, not just in themselves but in everything around them, especially their children. Children have so many holes in them, gaps and spaces, you can feel the wind whipping through their bodies. The role of women, he said, is to be completely present, to concentrate, see them as they are. But too many women act like tyrants (his hands grew cold on her belly as he said this, his lips white), refusing to act as mirrors to their children; instead, they bend their children to fit their own needs.

He also said that women shouldn't even try to do the things men do. Why bother? Men's things weren't important, compared with the deep, saturating acceptance women could pour down like rain. He said that when women were pregnant, they shouldn't drive; their eyes become unfocused.

At eight months pregnant, Carol did feel that her eyes were unfocused. They were like her hips, which were wobbly; like her whole self, which felt distended and huge, like a great fleshy pod holding, deep inside, that dark being covered in hair and white vernix.

Then a month passed and it was near her sister's birthday. Carol told him she wanted to drive to Toronto, to see this sister, but he said she shouldn't, it was too risky. "All right," she had said, "I'll take the train."

Any movement at all could upset the baby, he said. Cause a hemorrhage.

—

"That's horrible!" I interjected. "What did he expect—for you to sit and *do* nothing—just be pregnant?"

"Yes," she said. "I think that's what he did want."

—

But she wanted to see her sister, and she told him so. "If you're willing to put your child at risk," he said, "then go ahead." He wasn't surprised. This was what women did— they put their children at risk.

She stopped going to him after that. And the baby did turn over—on its own. Six weeks later Carol delivered Emma, a natural birth again, in the bed upstairs. Spring came, and with the excitement of the new baby Carol forgot about the doctor. Then one day Tony came home from Dalford and told her that he had seen Michael Hagopian in town, and that he looked terrible.

—

Carol took a sip of her tea and looked at me. "When I told my sister that it was just by coincidence that Tony ran into Michael in town, she said: 'There are *never* coincidences.'" She smiled in that rueful way she had, and all I could think was that I wasn't the first one to hear this story.

"I did start thinking about him then," she continued. "But mostly I pitied him—because he'd been so sad, talking about compassionate viewing, looking at me, at other women, studying our bodies, then condemning us.

"Then charges were laid against him by two former patients. They accused him of sexually harassing them in his office. His licence to practise was suspended, then taken away entirely. His wife left him—said he had been sexually inappropriate with his own children."

Carol took another sip of her tea. "The police came to his house. Arrested him, charged him. Eventually the charges were dropped—but on condition that he not see his children. All this news just filled the Valley. Tony would come home and tell about how people were taking sides, some defending him, calling him a miracle worker, others saying he was sexist, or worse—a pedophile, a sexual predator. I didn't know what to think."

I stood up—I couldn't help myself—and went to the window, looking in the direction of Michael Hagopian's house. I couldn't see a light, only the leafless maple trees with a few brown leaves at their tips, and some trembling aspen near the split-rail fence, their trunks covered with blown snow. New snow had been falling steadily, quietly, piling up on the porch rail. It was the kind you could brush away easily with the back of your hand.

"And this is the man you think about constantly?"

"I know. It doesn't make sense, does it?"

I wanted to say that he sounded horrible. But there was more to it.

"I think you have to see the whole thing backwards," Carol said. "Then it fits." She put her face in her hands, not from grief but as people do when they are thinking. Then she ran her fingers through her hair. "It's like any prophet. Nothing they say makes sense at first, because it hurts. *Leave everything. Follow me.* Do you think people wanted to do that? They hated Christ."

"This man isn't Christ, Carol. Not even close. He sounds like an extremely damaged person."

"Maybe."

She pushed back the blanket and went into the kitchen. When I went in, she was in front of the open fridge, staring down at the package of tofu dogs she held in her hand.

"For dinner," she said. "The children like them."

Emma cried out, waking from her nap, and Carol went upstairs.

I sat back down on the couch, leafed through a copy of *Mothering* magazine, then dumped it on the floor. I felt upset and also (this was the part I had trouble facing) passed over, because Carol had confided in her sister before she talked to me. This was typical: when I was in school I would choose a best friend, only to find out that she was best friends with somebody else.

The man was a misogynist—that's what I thought (knowing I might not think this quite so vehemently if Carol hadn't slighted me). But there was something else there, beyond my anger and feeling of diminishment. It was that concept of compassionate viewing. He called it compassionate viewing, but it wasn't. *If done right,* he had said. Perhaps he knew that he himself couldn't do it right. I could picture his indifferent, chilly eyes looking at me, taking me in, hating me even; moving down to my pubic hair, over my large, freckled thighs. I imagined how coldly his eyes would focus on my nipples. And it felt good to picture it. That was the truth.

What would he think of me? I imagined him entering

the room as I lay on the table, then telling me to leave, it was over between us. I would scrabble off the table and clutch at his knees, stark naked, begging to be looked at.

I picked up a plastic block from the floor. It had a round peg on one side, something to fit in another block's hole, causing glee in babies. Perhaps I should clear up while Carol was upstairs, surprise her with an organized living room. But why bother? It would be kind, of course; but I didn't feel like being kind.

I went into the kitchen and opened the refrigerator. I got out some goat's cheese, cut away a slab, wondering if it would be noticed, then cut away another. Then I pulled out the cold pot of pea soup, broke the congealed surface with a spoon and ate some hasty spoonfuls. I could hear Carol's footsteps upstairs, so I flattened the surface of the soup and slid the pot back into the fridge. I went back to the living room, and sat once more on the couch.

Carol came in and sat down, holding Emma. She pulled up her long-sleeved undershirt and began to feed the baby. Something tightened in me as I looked at Carol's breast, the long nipple slipping every now and then from the baby's mouth like a small finger.

"Feel her head," Carol whispered. It was sweaty. "She's like a hot water bottle." Carol slipped her nipple from the baby's slack mouth and rearranged the pillow behind her head.

"Neither of us moved.

"Eight days ago I went into the sugar bush. I don't know if I went to see him. But I think I probably did."

I felt my heart beating harder, though perhaps it was just from my proximity to the sleeping baby, full of milk, satiated and oblivious. I touched Emma's arm. She was so deeply asleep that it could be lifted and lowered, gently. Behind her ear I saw a crust of old milk, where Carol had neglected to clean.

—

Eight days ago Carol had gone for a walk in the sugar bush. Tony had left that morning for Zimbabwe. She felt light, glad to be alone. She walked across the field, through the gate, into the maple forest, which crackled with its burden of frozen sap. Leaves rustled on the topmost branches. Emma was in her baby carrier on Carol's back. Damian walked ahead, snowshoeing, but finding it difficult because the snow was crusty under its thin layer of powder. Soon she would have to unbuckle the snowshoes and carry them herself while Damian walked beside her.

The shot came fast, splintering a branch that cut her cheek, leaving a tail of blood. She plucked her son from the snowbank by his jacket, pulled him down beside her. *Shh,* she said—to everything he was about to do: cry, move, accuse her of hurting him. She unsnapped the baby carrier and swung Emma around, between her legs. Then she screamed outrage into the blue bush—screamed insults, swore, then stopped just as abruptly.

She stared past the trunks of the maples, across the undulating snow with its icy crust. Crystals floated in the air, burning her nostrils.

He came slowly, looking into the air two feet to the left of her. When he was close, he stopped. He held the rifle loosely in his right hand.

"Hello, Carol," he said, looking at the sky between the branches.

—

"He said *'Hello'* after he shot at you?"

"He didn't mean to shoot *at* me," Carol said. "He told me that afterwards. He just intended to shoot *near* me."

"He could have killed your children."

"I was angry. I know I swore bloody murder. But then—" She looked down at Emma in her lap. She stroked

131

her damp head absent-mindedly, and I thought for a moment that she was going to cry.

"I was angry," she said again. "But—"

"But what?"

—

But when he came forward, she saw the man she had known, the man who had touched her stomach, heated it. But he was changed now, gaunt, his neck sinewy. A tendon showed beneath his skin. He wore a flannel shirt, not nearly sufficient for the cold, and a pair of loose overalls. No gloves. His hands had frozen; his fingers were white at the tips. Yellow-white.

—

"Which is even worse," I said, "because if his fingers were numb, he might have fired a warning shot and hit you."

"If your fingers get that bad, you can lose them," Carol said.

—

She thought he might keep watching the sky until at last he raised his rifle, fixed her precisely in his sights and shot her through the head. She felt an old dream shudder in her. Blood on the snow.

She said whatever she could think of: *I know I'm in your bush, Michael. I know I'm not supposed to be.* She talked slowly, reassuringly.

Are your hands cold?

He had laughed then, as though that were a joke only he could get.

Why don't you come inside. I'll give you something warm.

—

"But did part of you think he really meant to kill you?"

Carol looked towards the window. "I never stopped thinking that," she said.

—

She led him across the snow crust, marked by her boot tracks and Damian's snowshoe prints. They went out of the maple bush, through the gate, towards the house. As she walked, she remembered her dream. A fox had killed a squirrel, then dragged its body into a hole. There was blood on the snow crystals. Pink, like frozen lemonade.

She put his hands in lukewarm water. In the basin, upstairs. She put his hands in, held them in. They looked down at them together. Her hands on top of his. Then she wrapped his hands in a warm towel.

The backs of his hands had dark hairs on them, and criss-crosses of lines. Delicate tips.

"Tony's away," he said.

—

"We sat right at that table. I gave him soup. Pea soup, the kind I gave you. He drank it. Wiped his mouth against his sleeve.

"I was afraid for him. I was—

"I came close to him, to clear away his soup mug. He pressed me towards him, hands against my back, so that I was between his legs. Then he lifted my shirt. Put his head against my belly."

—

Her stomach had gurgled, she remembered. His hair had felt soft against her belly.

That was it. That gesture. Ear to her stomach, listening. Her breasts above, milky, close. She put her hands on his head, and held him there.

—

Then he took the gun and left.

"I wanted him to take Tony's gloves," she said. "But he said he didn't wear other men's clothes."

As though it were a long-standing point of pride.

When she was done telling the story, I breathed out. Then Carol breathed out. She laid Emma carefully on the couch, stood up and turned on a lamp. She took hold of the curtain, but she didn't draw it. Instead, she looked out past the grove of trembling aspen, through the maple forest, to where a man was sitting by an unlit wood stove, a rifle across his legs. A man who had put his head against the tracery of stretch marks on her stomach. I knew she was imagining his pocked face, yellow fingertips, the black barrel of the gun—then seeing deeper, past his skin, into his porous bones, the lacework of veins and capillaries. And while she stood there, imagining him, he was doing the same thing to her: entering her, again and again, flooding her body.

In that moment I wanted that so badly for myself: to be knocked at, unloosened, to feel another person banging against me from the inside. It seemed, all at once, to be the one thing worth having. I felt an old closing sensation, a door shutting inside me but locking me out.

"You know you can't leave Tony," I said.

That was precisely what she was capable of: crossing the blue snow, opening the door to his freezing house, lifting her shirt to lay his head against her stomach, while with the other hand she pried his icy fingers from the trigger. Even if he refused, even if he grasped her by the hair and pressed the dark hole of the gun to her cheek, she would try to face him, willing him to look at her. Just look.

"Carol," I said. "You must promise me you won't go. *Promise me.*"

Then I saw that she was facing the window because she was crying. Her shoulders weren't heaving, she wasn't moving, but she was holding the sill, and her head was bowed.

"I'm not going to do anything," she said. "I have children."

I went over to her, where she stood by the window. I wanted her to cry onto me, perhaps even lay her head on my belly. But I knew she wouldn't do that. Still, I reached out for her, and she turned, dutifully, and let me hug her. She began to shake, then, while I stroked her blond hair, and the grey parts too, and felt her hot tears on my neck. *Like a baptism,* I thought, and hated myself for it, because I can never be in the moment, and so it was then: I was turning it into something it wasn't, into me being baptized by her tears.

terracotta

"BEAVER," Kurt said—then laughed.

Beaver. For some reason, when Kurt said it, Ned pictured a small, snorting animal, its nose pressed against the forest floor—something nocturnal and partially blind, like a badger or a hedgehog.

The moon had risen above the trees, brightening the clearing where the three boys sat. Ned was crouched against a stump while Kurt and Martin leaned against a log, smoking. Kurt held a piece of bark in the palm of his hand, a shaggy, dagger-shaped thing. He jabbed it into the ground. "Beaver-poking time soon," he said, and Ned imagined the beaver, dark with bristles, trying desperately to waddle back to the river.

Anger flooded Ned's stomach, flooded his bent knees, made his back tingle. It wasn't just Kurt, thin as a jackknife, glinting with foulness, that made him so furious; it was his older brother, Martin, sitting there in his Indian sweater, woolly as a sheepdog, compliant smiles breaking across his ruddy face. His cheek had three pimples on it. He smirked each time Kurt jabbed the bark into the ground and said something disgusting, just as though there were a string that pulled from that piece of wood up to Martin's slack, enjoying lips. As though nothing mattered more.

Martin and Kurt had finished a bottle of red wine—wine Ned had refused—and they were bleary and pleased with themselves, waiting for Suzette and Carla-ha-ha. Earlier, Kurt had said that Suzette had gone "all the way," not only with Kurt himself but with quite a few other boys as well, if you could believe them (which Ned didn't). Carla-ha-ha was Suzette's friend. She never spoke; she giggled.

"Want to know what it's like?" Kurt said now.

"Sure."

"It's fishy."

"Like tuna fish?"

"Like anchovies."

"That's gross."

"I know. I told you that. I told you it was gross. You're such an innocent, Marty."

"Martin." Ned spoke up suddenly. "He likes being called Martin, not Marty. Right, Martin?"

"It doesn't matter."

"Well, that's what you've always told me."

"He said it doesn't matter." Kurt glared at Ned, then went on. "You ever heard of sloppy seconds?"

"What's that?" Martin said.

"You don't know?"

"Why should I?"

"You're such an *innocent*, Marty," Kurt said again. "Sloppy seconds, man. Don't you ever watch porno flicks? It's when one guy does it, then another guy does it right after."

"What does that mean?"

"To a chick. Does it to a chick. Well, that's my idea for tonight. With Suzette. We do it twice, you know. Me, then you."

"What if she doesn't want to?"

"She will."

"What if she doesn't?"

"She will. What do you think she's coming to the woods for? She will, that's all. I know she will. She's into that kind of stuff, believe me."

Martin lit a cigarette. He saw Ned watching him and wished, with a vehement exhalation, that he hadn't brought him. It was like having his mother there, or someone even older than his mother—a beetling old lady with a scarf over her head and glassy, appalled eyes.

The moon like a blind and open eye.

Ned had been making up those words earlier that

night, his cheek laid against the cool windowsill. The words had soothed him, but he couldn't say why. The sensation was similar to those moments before he fell asleep, when words floated up in a hidden order.

Once, he had seen a white elephant, its flank smooth as a greased egg, swell up towards him, then stampede down a tunnel. *I have seen the forever elephant,* he had thought, and those words seemed, for a brief second, to express everything there was in this world—and parts beyond the world as well.

Martin had come in and found him there at the window, his chin sunk in his hand.

"Come on," he had insisted in the old way. Not the way he was with Kurt nowadays—lost and snorting at every dirty joke—but the way he used to be, back when Martin would coax Ned to come fishing, before dawn. They would take their father's wooden boat, motoring silently up the Sound to that mysterious place called Hole-in-the-Wall, where the salmon came in huge schools. Their shadowed bodies passed under the boat, moving in one direction, then turning—a single, skittish entity.

"Come on," Martin said in that old big-brotherish way. "You'll have a good time. Let's get out." Ned's strangeness gave Martin a familiar tug of worry down in his stomach.

"What'll we do?" Ned said.

"I don't know. What does it matter? You're not doing anything now."

The moon like a mother with its stillborn child
Pressed in rags against its side.

Now Ned sat watching his brother and Kurt from his place in the shadows.

"And guess what it feels like?" Kurt was asking.

Martin shrugged.

"Come on. Guess."

Martin closed his eyes and snorted.

"It feels like chopped liver."

Ned had never felt chopped liver, but he could imagine. It was red, like kidney, with a film of blue skin on top.

"Stop it," he said, and amazingly both Kurt and Martin stopped. Ned's head was raised, his too bright eyes glinting. "You're being disgusting."

"What's wrong with him?" Kurt said.

"I don't know."

Ned turned on Martin. "I can't believe you go along

with him." He stood up and glared at them, like a snake about to strike.

Martin sighed and pushed himself up. "Come here." He took Ned by the arm and, with a shrug back at Kurt, walked his brother to the edge of the clearing. "Look," he said, "I brought you here because I thought you'd have some fun. Now don't embarrass me."

"Me, embarrass you! Look how you're acting. You're being sick, Martin."

"No, I'm not. Not by a long shot."

"You'd actually think of doing things so—so—" Ned couldn't find the word to express his disgust. "—so bad," he said. "What kind of person are you? I feel like I don't even *know* who you are any more." He pulled himself away from his brother's hand and ran out of the clearing.

"Well, maybe you should learn," Martin said, but too softly for Ned to hear.

Ned was too old to run back to his mother; but that was what he was doing. What he knew he shouldn't do, but did anyway—through the forest, past the muddy stream.

Certain words meant his mother. *Amphora. Terracotta.* The whole of India was his mother, because that was where she had been born, and where she had lived, early on, at the very beginning, before she was uprooted. There were so many twists to her past—Vancouver, then London, then far, far back, India—that you had to be vigilant to find your way back to the source, and you could get lost down corridors. *Amphora. Terracotta. Labyrinth. Shiva.* The darkness of her skin was like earth and sand. He thought of this as he ran out of the forest and onto the road lit by street lamps.

Once, she had told him her earliest memory: she had looked out a window and seen women passing by on the road underneath. Their dusky bodies were covered in blazing turquoise, purple and saffron saris, like a flood of peacocks. Every time he thought of this, he had the same startling revelation, the same thrill, until now it was his earliest memory too.

He would run home and in the still house they would sit on the couch together, their bare feet propped on the chest with the brass corners, their toes all in a row, teacups resting on their stomachs. It would be hard to tell whose toes were whose; their skin was the same dusty colour, with an underwash of mauve.

"Something's wrong," she would say.

"No."

But she would discern. "You're angry with Martin."

And he would find words to say all that sat in a lump against his throat. "He doesn't act right. He's not who he really is any more."

"Don't worry about Martin," she would say. "He'll come back."

And there they would be in the room with its wood-panelled walls, in the eye, the circle of stillness, to which Martin, inevitably, would return.

As he passed each street lamp, his shadow shortened to an ape's length, burly and dwarfish, then it grew and thinned and shot out, melted into light, and was replaced again by the stump likeness of his running feet.

He was a hundred feet from the driveway when he stopped running. His body remembered first, as though it were sick. His mother wasn't waiting. The spinning pea-cock colours weren't there. What he was running to was an absence that made the street glint, picking out flecks of mica, dots of tar, a puddle covered with a seep of mud. Under the street lamp, on the spread of gravel, was Earle Gilette's lavender Volkswagen—the same colour as the taste in Ned's throat. This was the car in which Earle had driven Ned home from school, with its bottle of vodka under the seat, and two metal cups, and Tang crystals. Martin had said they were there so that Earle could offer drinks to women, when he drove them up to the lookout on Cypress Mountain, at night, to look down at the lights of Vancouver.

Theirs was a post-and-beam cedar house, shoebox-shaped, with a chimney on one end, a porch on the other, and trees casting shade with sloping branches, the exact droop and arch of which Ned had tried to write poems about.

The cedars sway their full arms down.

The branches knew what he felt. Something foul and grey, a rat's nest, was lodged at the centre of his home.

In the dining room his mother had laid two plates on the table close by one another, and a candle, and the linen napkins with the white brocade, the English napkins from her father's side of the family. Ned looked into the living room and saw Earle leaning back on the couch, his belly bulging over his belt, his fingers spread on his thighs. He was laughing at something Ned's mother had just said.

"Ned!" She rose. She was wearing a burgundy dress with gold, sparkling threads sewn through it, one he had never seen. "Ned, you're home. Are you hungry?"

"Hey, Ned!" Earle called out with cowboy jocularity.

His mother came and looked him in the eye, then

leaned down and kissed his forehead. "I thought you went out with Martin."

"I did." He could feel the warmth she gave off from various places: her stomach, her forearms, her cheeks.

"And?"

"He wanted to do things I didn't want to do."

"Ah."

"He was with Kurt," Ned said.

"Who's Kurt?" That was Earle, butting in, his pink face turned to them.

"Kurt is Martin's friend," his mother said.

"An unsavoury influence?"

"I suppose you could say that. Last weekend he and Martin came home at three in the morning."

Earle rolled his head back and laughed. "Boys will be boys."

"I suppose."

"Oh, you can count on it, Sereta, I know."

His mother's face was lit with something fantastical. What was it? It was pleasure at this pig-man parked on the couch, giving out hints on raising boys. She had turned to Earle for reassurance, and now she was meeting his platitudes with grateful radiance, as though he handed her jewels to place between her teeth. Her lips were red with lipstick. Her eyes were lined with Egyptian pencil.

Earle said, "I hope, now that you're here, you'll stay for my beef stroganoff. I make the best beef stroganoff—"

"He does—"

But Ned didn't listen further. He turned and ran to his bedroom, slamming the door.

On his desk was a model of *Apollo XI*, which he had been making painstakingly, for too long. He picked it up with both hands and raised it over his head, wanting to fling it onto the tiled floor. He would have liked to see the plastic bits, so faithfully stuck together with epoxy, broken and scattered.

His mother's knuckles made a whispery knock at his door. "Neddy?"

He wanted to believe she had come as she used to, to extricate the black ache in his heart, to ease it out gently, as one might ease a sliver from a hurt finger. He sat on his bed, his shoulders slumped, still holding the rocket ship in both hands.

"May I come in?"

He said nothing, and she turned the knob and entered. She switched on the overhead light, and the threads of her dress gleamed as she sat down beside him.

"What's wrong, dear?"

He shook his head.

She stroked his hair, the down of his neck, and he let her do it. Then, against his will, he let her lower his head into her lap. "You're unhappy, darling. I can see. Tell me why."

He tried to say what Martin and Kurt were going to do. He waited for the words to form themselves, to rise up and be spoken, but then he noticed her palms were clammy and hot. Too hot. And she was bumping his earlobe as she rubbed. Her breath had an ether-like undertone of vodka, and from her lap, that fertile delta, something too ripe. Words he didn't invite blossomed, each one perfect and foul, spoken with Kurt's chemical leer. He opened his eyes to see her stroking his head, lost in the rhythm, her lips wet with lipstick.

"Why aren't you out there with Earle?" he said, sitting up.

"I wanted to find out what was wrong."

"You don't want to keep him waiting."

"He's all right waiting for a little while. He understands."

"He understands!"

She reached out for him.

"You've been drinking," he said. "I hate it when you drink."

"Oh, Ned!" She smiled tipsily, wanting reassurance. She was not herself any more; she was the vacant, dispossessed presence she became when she drank. Her eyes had the spark missing in them, and she groped forward to touch him.

He sprang back, dropped the *Apollo XI*, and it broke under his foot.

"Oh, Ned!" she cried again, blind and maudlin. She got down on her knees to pick up the pieces.

"You're a drunken bitch," he whispered, shocked at what came from him.

She raised her stricken mouth, open in an O. He started for the door, but there was Earle, big as a white boar on its hind legs, bristling, blocking the exit. Ned ran to the window, pushed it open and slid through as Earle clutched at the back of his shirt. Ned tore around the house and down the driveway, gravel spraying up from his soles.

—

Martin lay back and looked at the upside-down trees, the round and pulsing moon. "And people have walked there," he said. "Hard to believe."

Suzette blew smoke from both sides of her mouth. "One giant step for man."

"I'd like to do that."

"What?"

"Fly up in a spaceship, you know. Look down on Earth."

"Warp Nine, Scotty," Kurt said.

Carla laughed. She sat cross-legged, stalwart and heavy-looking in her lumberjack shirt, her skin the colour of tallow. "It's supposed to be really different from up there," Martin said. "All that black space, and you look back and there's one spot of green and blue colour."

"Yeah," Suzette said. "I've heard that too." She was wearing tight jeans and a clinging, elasticized shirt with small pink roses on it. Her breasts rose up white in the dark. She lay back and looked at the sky. "It keeps bobbing," she giggled. She and Carla had arrived with half a mickey of gin, which they had shared with the boys.

Carla stood up and walked down the path at the edge of the clearing. She found a huckleberry bush and began to eat, pulling the branch down with her hand, then picking the berries off with her teeth.

"What are you doing?" Kurt asked.

Carla giggled.

"Eating berries?"

"Uh-huh."

"Let's go hunt for some more."

They foraged away, Kurt holding back the branches for her, a gentleman of the forest, while Carla lumbered behind.

Suzette lay beside Martin, her freckles standing out like small dapples—hints of disquiet—on her face. Her eyes were Chinese in their length, sloped and dreamy.

"I'd like to fly up in a spaceship," he continued. "I'd like to see what it would be like to step right onto it."

"Not me. I like it here."

"Or even fly past it."

"To see Mars."

"Jupiter."

"Or fly into a black hole and come out yesterday."

"Yeah."

The fear he had with girls was gone. He could see her body on the ground near his own. Her lips looked blue or red, he couldn't tell which. She was both frozen and voluptuous, and he saw that her voluptuousness was something she didn't want to have, but which she wore flagrantly for that very reason.

"Are you cold?"

"A little."

"Do you want my sweater?"

"What a gentleman. No, I'm fine, thanks. Kurt's got the hots for Carla tonight."

"Seems like it. Are you mad?"

"I don't care. Let him. All guys are jerks, anyway."

Martin lit two cigarettes in his mouth—how had he gotten so good at this?—and passed one to her. She was talking about her stepfather now.

"I fucking hate him," she said.

"Why?"

"You wouldn't want to know." A depth of hurt lay beneath her skin. "He's a fucking pervert, that's all." She blew her smoke upwards in rings. "How about you? What's your old man like?"

"He's dead."

"I'm sorry."

"Oh, don't worry. It happened five years ago. I'm used to it now."

"Still…"

"He drowned. He was in a submersible. He used to do that—underwater exploration. He was in a submersible and it didn't come up, the radio cut off, the propeller was caught in reeds."

"Do you miss him?"

"Yeah. Sometimes." He thought about it, looking up at the space between the trees. "Yeah. A lot. I don't think Ned does as much. I don't think Ned remembers him as much as I do."

"That's really sad."

"Yeah. Well…"

"These things happen," she said.

"That's right," he echoed. "They happen."

They breathed out smoke together.

Her eyelids were veined and pale as moth wings. In daylight, Martin remembered, at school, her blue eyes had a frightening marble clarity; but they were soft now, veiled with shadows, as though all that they contained in daytime could be let go. Her face looked pure in the moonlight, but underneath, like a second bobbing image of the moon, he saw another Suzette—an inner, angry self— beating against the walls of her skin. This self said, *My step-father's an asshole.* It said, *My stepfather's a pervert.* It blew smoke in contempt at the moon. Both images of Suzette held him in trance, but it was this second, beating, angry self that seemed most lovely.

"You're really beautiful," he said. "Do you know that?"

She snorted.

"Really." He sat up. "Your skin in the moonlight is really beautiful. I've been looking at it all the time. It's like—it's so white and clear—"

She snorted again.

"Really. You're beautiful, Suzette."

"I'm not beautiful."

"Yes, you are. You're really unusual. I've never seen anyone who looks like you. All those freckles—"

"You see!"

"—against that white skin—" He grasped her hand. "You don't know you're beautiful, do you? You don't know you're beautiful."

"I don't think I am."

"You are."

He wanted to reach out and touch her cheek, and then he found that he had, and that she had raised her lips and he was kissing her. It was his first kiss, though nobody, not even Ned and certainly not Kurt, knew this. He found that it came easily, that he was certain and able, and her lips touching his were chaste and cool.

From the dark there was a patter of pine cones, then a catcall.

"What was that?" Suzette asked.

"It's Kurt. Getting jealous." He kissed her again.

"Oh baby—" A falsetto voice broke across the clearing. "Oh baby." Then the sound of panting.

"They're spying on us."

"That's so immature," Suzette called out.

Stick it where the sun don't shine, Marty,
Stick it where the sun don't shine.
Fifteen men on a dead man's raft,
Stick it where the sun don't shine."

"Ned," Martin called, chilled suddenly. "Is that you?" But the voice was like a tiger's in a jungle, coming from all directions. Martin got up and began to look around the edge of the clearing, thrashing clumsily at the fronds of ferns.

"Yoo-hoo," the voice called. "Over here." Martin stumbled towards it. "Over here," it breathed. "No, not there. Over here."

"He doesn't sound right," Martin said.

"Full fathom five, thy father lies—"

"Neddy! Where are you?"

"And of his bones are coral made—"

"Neddy!"

"Look." Suzette pointed upward. Twenty-five feet in the air, balancing on the branch of a cedar, was Ned, his body lit with radiance.

"Ned!" Martin called in relief. "How did you get up there?"

"How do you think? I flew."

"I thought you'd gone home."

"So did I."

"Come down now. It's not safe."

Ned let go of the trunk and stood on the branch, bobbing, then grasped the trunk again.

"He's pissed," Suzette said.

"He doesn't drink."

"He's holding a bottle."

Martin heard the clink of a bottle knocked against teeth.

"Are you drinking something?" Martin called.

"Vodka."

"Where'd you get it?"

"From Earle's car. Hey, Kurt," he called out as Kurt came into the clearing. "Hey Carla-ha-ha-ha-ha-ha-ha."

"Who's up there?" Kurt asked.

"It's the boy wonder," Suzette said. "Martin's brother. And he's got a bottle of vodka."

"Ned, old boy." Kurt's voice was unctuous. "Come on down and share that around."

Branches shifted, Ned disappeared, there was thrashing,

then Ned hung by one arm from the bottommost branch. He swung in the air, then fell into a simian squat on the ground, the bottle raised above his head like a prize coconut.

"Vodka," Kurt whispered. "Pass it around, Ned old boy." He went to take it, but Ned tucked the bottle to his chest.

"Wait," Ned said. He sat down on the log and Suzette sat beside him. He was invincible; he felt that in the extreme liquid ease of his body, the warmth in his stomach, making all that he did languid and perfect. All around him things had a clean, whistling edge, as though they'd been scraped clear of the dust, the grey taste they had in waking life.

He passed the bottle to Suzette and she drank deeply, then handed it to Martin, who sat down beside her on the log. After taking a drink, he passed it along to Carla, who stood in front of him, a solid, dark presence in her jeans and lumberjack shirt. She poured the vodka into her mouth, then smacked her lips and shivered and laughed. Kurt drank greedily.

"So," Ned said when the bottle came back to him, "what about it?"

"What about what?"

"What we're here for."

"What's that?" Suzette laughed.

"Come on, Martin, tell her."

"I don't know what you're talking about."

Ned leaned over Suzette and whispered something to Martin, who snorted in contempt. "Don't," he said.

"What did he say?" Suzette asked.

"Nothing. Don't pay attention to him."

"Marty and Kurt want to play a few games, right?" Ned said this in a high, teasing voice that Martin had never heard.

"Just ignore him."

"What kind of games?" Suzette said. "I want to play. Come on, what kind of games?"

"It's nothing," Martin said, but Ned turned his hard brilliance away from his brother and smiled again at Suzette, who was lighting a cigarette.

"Can I have one?" he asked.

"Sure." She stuck the cigarette in the side of his mouth and lit it.

"You don't smoke," Martin said.

"No? Well, I do now."

"So what's this game you're talking about?" Suzette said.

"It's nothing." Martin gazed at the ground.

"It was a dare game," Kurt said easily. "Do you do dares?"

"Of course we do. Right, Carla?"

Ned held the bottle out to Suzette. "I dare you to finish the bottle."

"That's easy." She stood and raised the bottle to her lips, her swanlike neck poised. She drank ten swift gulps. When she was done, she held out the bottle to them all and let it smash against a rock. "Done," she smiled. "Done. Now don't say I don't do what I say I'll do. Now don't say it," she said. "Who's next?"

"Carla," Kurt said.

"Take off your clothes, Carla." Suzette held back her head and laughed, then she leaned forward. "Come on, Carla," she commanded, waving her arm. "Take 'em off."

Carla giggled and shook her head.

"Oh, fuck it. Don't be such a prude."

"You don't have to," Martin said.

Suzette turned on him. "And you! You're a prude, too. Watch me," she said. "I've at least got guts." She pulled her shirt over her head and her breasts bobbed in the soft, plush bra. Then she stood and unbuttoned her jeans, taking three faulty steps to the right. She straightened herself and pulled down her pants, unpeeled them, then kicked the tangled legs off her ankles. She wore clinging purple satin underwear.

"There," she said, as though settling a score. "I've got to lie down. I'm really dizzy." She aimed at the earth and hit it, then rolled over on her back.

The three boys and Carla looked at her. She had her hands over her eyes, her back arched against the dry leaves, her long legs freckled like dotted stone. Even her toes were tense, holding her rigid body up above the leaves. She groaned.

Martin, watching from his perch on the log, saw the satin underwear, and her belly button, and the shape of her pelvic bones framing her belly. She groaned again. As Martin watched, Kurt got down on the ground and found the fastening of her bra between her breasts and opened it. Her breasts came out, loose and white. It was like a performance to see the dark-haired boy down on his knees by the head of the moaning girl. Ned watched too, and then he found he could not sit still any longer. He too was down on the ground, his hand touching the slippery underwear, feeling the silk and heat between her legs. She thrashed her head back and forth in the leaves. He pulled down the sides of her underwear and there was the earth-tone mound, the terracotta mound of hair.

"Touch it," Kurt said, a voice in Ned's inner ear. Ned touched the two lips with his fingers, found their parting and pressed them open.

She convulsed slightly, a shiver running up her body. Martin watched as his brother again touched the place between her freckled legs.

"Stop," Suzette called out, gritting her teeth. Her eyes opened. "Stop it," she said clearly.

"Do it," Kurt hissed.

Ned slid his finger deep, as deep as he could. She kicked, and Ned pinned her legs under his knees. Suzette flailed, found her voice, tried to sit up, but Kurt pressed her mouth to form a bee-stung kiss that stopped her voice.

Then there was a shape, a furious blurred shape rising out of the woods. It picked Ned up like a black stick and held him in the air, his arms dangling. *Hey, hey, hey,* it yelled, and twirled him and he flew. Then it turned on Martin, and he saw it was Carla risen up on her hind legs, her face raw with fury. He backed away from her and lifted his hands. He heard boughs breaking, roots cracking, as Kurt ran howling into the woods.

Then Suzette was up too, screaming into Martin's face. She screamed three times, then raked her fingernails down his cheeks. He tried to shield himself, and when he opened his eyes, the two girls—one naked, one dark—were disappearing into the woods at a limping jog.

—

The moon like a blind and opened eye
Stared down at them from the edge of the sky.

Ned lay face down. The fall replayed itself in a stream of falling and landings, punctuated by blackness.

When he looked up, he found the forest screaming with birds and dawn light. He saw Martin asleep beside a log, his legs pulled up in a fetal position, the crack of his bum showing above his jeans. Ned rested his cheek on the leaves, and slept.

He woke again when burning liquid shot from his throat, steaming onto the ground. He crumpled down, hiding his eyes from the stabbing sun, then felt the weight of Martin's arm, neither drawing Ned to him nor holding him away, but steadying him.

"Let's go," Martin said at last, when Ned had stopped heaving. But Ned would not go.

"How could I do that?" Ned said.

Martin looked at his brother's wan face, the smell of spewed vodka rising from his jeans. He remembered through shards that had split apart, some hidden, some piercing, the freckled face of Suzette raised to the moon. He was afraid of what else he would remember as the day grew longer and the heat advanced, but for now he said, "It's all right," and he stroked his hand a little way down his brother's sloped shoulder. "It's all right," he repeated. And because it was what *she* had said, he added: "These things happen."

the chlorine flower

IT WAS A YOUNG MAN, a new employee, who first saw
the shimmering object float to the surface of the vat. He
thought it was an air bubble. But although it trembled
lightly, it did not pop. He called to the other men, and they
said it looked like a clump of waste. It was only when it had
risen above the bubbling yellow chemicals, and the men
saw its eye-shaped leaves, its ghostly stem, its glowing skin-
like petals, that they realized, all at once, that it was a flower.

They watched it all morning as it floated above the
vat, glistening and growing more or less vivid depending
on the vapours rising from the boiling chlorine. When the
foreman came in to announce the ten o'clock break, he
poked at the flower with a long metal pole used to stir the
vat, noting that the flower was weightless, insubstantial.

Five assistant engineers reported to the site. They told
each other that it must be a mass delusion caused by
stress, or fumes, or a trick of light. But when they turned
off the breaker switch, the flower reappeared like a ghost's
hand, vein and bone and vaporous flesh, and so they
decided it was caused by deviant chlorine crystals, which
had aggregated to cast a flower shadow, like a slide

projection. It glowed, though, even after they had drained the chlorine from the pool, radiating at the edges of each daisy petal, rising up as tall as a man from the floor of the concrete basin.

The chemical factory squatted next to a large lake, in the industrial suburbs of a small town in Saskatchewan. Its smoked-glass windows glinted in the sun like the many eyes of a fly. Inside, it was constructed of gradually tightening circles, with senior management offices on the outside, the cubicles for assistant managers and clerical staff in the middle, and the mixing rooms, drainage cellars and chemical storage rooms at the centre. There was such a hum from the vat room that the men who unlocked its door each morning felt they were entering the chamber of a warm heart.

The vat-room workers and assistant engineers leaned against the lime-stained wall and sat on the bench. The newest employee noticed that the flower had a scent. The others agreed. It tickled the roof of each mouth with a lemon taste and smelled fresh, like bleached shirts on a clothesline. For a long time the assistant engineers and vat workers raised their faces toward the emptied basin, their noses twitching. The flower glowed more brightly, the follicles on its stem catching the light like needles of ice.

The head of senior management was notified of the work stoppage. He received a briefing on events, then went to the site to order the men back to work.

"Well, what have we here," he said, sniffing, displeased. He climbed into the empty vat to examine the flower. Passing his hand through its translucent stem, he noticed that the light on his skin refracted in rainbows, that the flower felt soft and seemed to caress his skin, and that the stem was not uniformly white or clear, but was bathed in a soft, promising pink as though flushing with pleasure. A flutter of dust specks rose up the slender column of its stem.

He took off his gloves and touched it with his fingers. It felt warm and very pleasant. He took off his surgical mask and washed his face in the light cast upward by the stem. At once there was not a man in the crowded room who didn't want to take off his surgical mask and gloves too, and bathe his skin in the light of the flower. They took turns, playing checkers as they waited, their legs dangling into the empty pool. The petals of the flower, which had at first seemed so immaterial, had become—or perhaps had always been but now were showing themselves to be—marbled through with soft pink, like veins showing discreetly through skin.

The president of the chemical corporation was sitting at his desk, staring at the lake, a leather-bound book on epiphenomenalism the only object on his desk. He was wistful for the days when he had had chemical formulae to formulate, but he had long ago delegated any tasks that required moving from his desk to more junior levels of management.

The senior manager knocked at his door. "There's an ongoing incident in the vat room," he said.

"Ah," said the president. "Indeed." He scratched his ear.

"You should come, sir, and see."

What a relief to stride down the hallway with a sense of purpose. As he neared the vat room, he saw a crowd of workers silhouetted in the pale light streaming through the opened door. He walked into the room frowning, as if to say, "Now you will have me to deal with." Some men smiled and cocked their heads, but others simply gestured, without speech, to the centre of the vat. The president turned and saw the flower.

It was a daisy. It was not necessary to tell him, he could already see. If it had been a ghost magnolia, or an aching tropical orchid, he would have been moved, but not like this; nothing could be like this. There could only be one such moment, one such flower, and there it was. It rose toward the ceiling absurdly out of place, eloquent, trembling, perhaps even nearsighted; and he remembered his mother whose death he had never mourned, whom he had last seen standing on the sidewalk, looking absurd and eloquent and nearsighted with her white piqué hat tilted to one side, while he drove away with his father and never came back. The flower's porcelain petals opened to reveal its dark disk, which trembled with currents of air as though moved at the centre of its being. But this dark disk, which seemed at first like the eye of any daisy, was in fact a velvety cavern, a tunnel, stained with a flush of purple and soft as the throat of a petunia.

Several men brought the president a stepladder. He propped it beside the daisy's gleaming shaft and climbed up, trembling. He raised his hand and stroked the flower's shadowy mouth. Then all the men knew how much they wanted, had wanted all their lives, to stroke its tender inner tunnel. The newest employee thought he heard it hum, a throaty, intimate moan of pleasure. The senior manager remembered his dead son and began to weep, seeing such brilliance at the end of the dark channel.

They took turns all day and far into the night, climbing the ladder, stroking the flower, telling stories, while soft murmurs rose from its centre.

At dawn the flower's petals and stem vanished. Its disk glowed for several hours like a sunspot, then faded away. The men took the long pole and poked softly at the air. Nothing trembled or glinted.

"You must all have the day off," the president said, "to mark its coming and going."

It was hard to leave the site, but at last the men dispersed, driving down the empty freeway toward the city. But the president himself walked across the yellow fields of corn stubble to the lake. For an instant he wanted to set out barefoot across the prairie, crossing fields, carrying a message that he would scatter like new seed. But here he stopped, because he couldn't say what the message was.

I have seen, he would say, *a flower grow from a chlorine basin.*

But did this mean that everyone should stop doing what they were doing, for the sake of the flower, or did it mean not to worry, never to worry, because the flower could grow through anything? Did the flower mean, as he had felt at the time, that his mother had always wanted him, or—here he stopped—had she returned only to say that she was gone, and this time for good? Bathed in these doubts, he felt the force of the chlorine flower draining away. He remembered a young man standing beside him most of the night. "Speak again, bright angel," the man had whispered near dawn, as the flower faded. The president said these words now, but the world was silent, the lake was perfectly still, and not a ripple passed across its surface to tell him what to do.

bare-breasted women

WOMEN ARE PLANNING to take off their shirts and parade down Main Street. It's become the thing to do. It started in Guelph—where a young woman was arrested for indecent exposure when she took off her shirt and walked down the street—then spread to Toronto, and now it has shot across the country to Vancouver and Victoria, and somehow even to this last small-town outpost in the Okanagan Valley.

Ruth laughs as she and her daughter Gloria discuss it while they make supper. They are making the gravy together. Or Ruth is making the gravy and Gloria is sitting on the radiator talking to her. Ruth is a woman of sixty-three, with salt-and-pepper hair cut close around her face, and a flap of skin beneath her chin that she tugs at sometimes, calling it her wattle. Her skin is yellow and tired-looking on her neck, liver-coloured and tough on her cheeks, caused mainly by high blood pressure and having smoked too many cigarettes for too long. She is a pleasantly plump woman, with nice curves still, although much of her extra weight has accumulated around her stomach. Still, she would rather, she has explained to Gloria, her twenty-three-year-old eco-feminist daughter, far rather carry a little extra poundage than end up looking gaunt.

What Ruth likes best about the story, which she read that day in the *Penticton Herald*, is that there has been a counter-demonstration called. In Penticton a contingent of women will descend on their naked sisters and cover them with tablecloths and blankets. Gloria doesn't find this amusing.

"Why should men be allowed to go naked from the waist up and women not be able to?" she complains from the radiator. "It doesn't strike me as fair. Women are *so* defined by our sexuality and our bodies, so held back because of how other people perceive us. Why not just take off your shirt if you're hot? Why not do it, just as a man would? I think if the majority of women just did it, then men's ridiculous attitudes towards our bodies would have to change. They'd have to stop seeing breasts as sex symbols—"

"It will take a lot more than demonstrations." Geoffrey, Gloria's father, calls this from the screened-in porch that adjoins the kitchen, where he sits reading the newspaper. And this silences Gloria, who didn't know her father had been listening. It isn't that she shies away from a good political fight—she and her father have one at practically every meal—it's just that she cannot talk about breasts in her father's presence without blushing.

"It's a touchy subject," Ruth says.

"You're telling me," Geoffrey says. "You've hit it right on the head there, darling."

Ruth pulls on her oven mitts and winks at Gloria. Then she takes the platter of roast beef from the oven and carries it to the table.

At dinnertime Geoffrey baits his daughter.

"How many radical feminists does it take to change a light bulb?"

"I don't know," she says, looking nervously down at the beet on her plate, cutting its smooth red flesh.

"That's not funny," Geoffrey says.

That's the punchline. Because feminists are supposed to have no humour. They are grim, dressed in black like their grandmothers, who wore massive navy blue bloomers. They meet in small rooms, these grim, butchy women, and plan world domination.

Gloria laughs, one sharp bark. "That's funny," she says. But Ruth can see the look on her daughter's face, and she knows Gloria doesn't think it's all that funny.

Too many of their political arguments end in silence

or tears. Geoffrey, a negotiator for a large coastal timber company, knows precisely how to goad Gloria until she lashes out at him.

Ruth is aware that the meal has started badly; that's why she sits at her end of the table with a smile clamping her jaw, a slightly feverish cheerfulness in her eyes, as though to indicate that whatever happens, whatever is said, she at least is prepared to smooth it over.

Her daughter has beautiful auburn hair, which she keeps short, and white skin with blue tints in the shadows, skin she inherited from Ruth's mother. She is almost six feet tall. But when she and Geoffrey have these arguments, she grows slope-shouldered, scrunches over, and eats without seeming to see her food. She isn't so much eating, Ruth thinks, as stoking herself. While Geoffrey is like a sea urchin all covered in black prickles, each prickle with a legal sheathing. He talks to Gloria as if negotiating a difficult deal on softwood lumber—one where he is determined, once and for all, to nail the opposition to the floor. He forgets who she is. He doesn't see she wants comfort from him, that she is attempting to reach through his prickles to touch the flesh between.

And when he has finally stung and pinned her, hurt her and fended her off—seeing her not so much as herself but as a horde of dogs perhaps, a horde of female dogs bent at getting at his soft stomach—then and only then will he stop thundering and come back into himself. He will look at Gloria staring stolidly down at the grain of the table, and he will be chagrined to discover he has hurt her, and he will give Ruth a sheepish smile as if to say, "But how could I help it? It was in self-defence."

Then it will be up to Ruth to apply her particular balms: a bowl of ice cream brought to Geoffrey after dinner, when he sits in the garden, brooding and smoking and drinking in the night scent of his rose bushes; a kiss on his forehead to say, *I know you didn't mean to go so far.* Then later, in the kitchen, she will talk to Gloria about how much her father loves her, underneath it all.

"Well, I say good for the demonstrators," Gloria is saying now. "Good for them. It's exactly what's called for. Women *should* join together and say, 'These are our bodies, our breasts.' They aren't sex symbols that have to be hidden away. They aren't lewd—so lewd a woman should be arrested for showing hers in public. Why can't a woman take off her shirt if she's hot? Because of the small-minded, snickering attitudes of men. No, worse than that: because it's a male-dominated society, a whole apparatus that exercises control over women."

"Darling—" Geoffrey always calls his daughter "darling" when he gets heated up. "Darling, what you say is utter rot—and I say that respectfully, of course. There is no grand plot amongst men to keep women decently clothed. We simply ask the same thing of all members of the species: that we cover ourselves up, for warmth, and for decency, and to stop the opposite sex from staring and all the rest that goes with staring. It's too much—" he flares suddenly into a real heat, "—just too much for women to think they can prance about semi-naked and not have men so much as notice."

Ruth knows this anger in Geoffrey. He is trying to wriggle out of a straitjacket, to trumpet a simple and basic biological truth—against the leagues of politically correct women who would bleed him of this right. And what he says is true, she thinks. Of course the female body excites men. How blind of these women to believe they can change men at their root. But she can also see that what Geoffrey has said embarrasses Gloria, and that the weight of her breasts, which she is so very self-conscious about, makes her daughter blush suddenly.

"But why do men have to stare?" Gloria says softly.

"Because we're human," Geoffrey thunders. "My God, we're human—and that's the trouble with all these demonstrators. They want to remake us all—turn us into another species, where the female body inspires nothing in men but the most solemn, devotional prayers. But I'm telling you—Ruth, don't look at me like that, I'm not going too far—when men see a pair of big naked knockers, they just naturally tend to stare."

Gloria lifts her pale face and meets her father's eyes and says: "That's because you think you have the right. But you don't, you know. Those knockers, as you call them, belong to someone else, not to you at all. Someone with a soul inside, and a mind. Someone who may not want to be stared at."

"You're too serious, Gloria."

"It is serious."

"Well, go on—be that way. I for one am going to smoke a cigarette in the garden. No, Ruth, I don't want ice cream."

They were summering in the Okanagan, Ruth and Geoffrey and Gloria. Gloria joined her parents most years, flying back from Toronto to Vancouver and meeting them at their house in the British Properties. Then they would drive up to the Okanagan Valley together, through the Fraser Valley, through Manning Park and past Princeton, leaving the coast behind, its rain forest and dripping, swollen foliage, coming into the spare, dusty heat of the interior.

Every year as Ruth passed out of the coastal mountains and into the heat of the lodgepole pine forests, then into the Okanagan with its dry hills and clutches of fertile orchards, she felt herself coming nearer to her dead mother. She came nearer as they drove through Summerland, along the highway that rimmed the western edge of the lake, then up the driveway towards the house with its screened-in, sagging front porch—a house, like many of the old houses in the valley, with a foundation of river rock. Ruth drew closer and closer to her mother, but in the last instance, as they drove up the driveway, it wasn't her mother who welcomed her, but the loss, the stillness that had always been there since her mother's death. And when she felt that loss, she knew it was what she had been driving towards all the time. The loss hung on everything, the loss which had been so bitter but which, twenty years later, she almost felt welcomed her.

The house nestled between two folds of orchard hillside, their pears on one slope, their neighbour's grapevines on the other. The land west of the farm was arid, but to the east a cool breeze blew up from the lake, moving through the pear leaves, rustling the poplar windbreak.

Geoffrey parked beside the enormous willow tree at the front, a tree planted when the house was first built. Over seventy years its roots had wormed their way between the foundation rocks, shifting them, causing the porch floorboards to sag. A few blind ends, like potato eyes, had even broken through the plaster of the cellar wall. Ruth had noticed them last summer when she went down to get a jar of pickles.

They each took a suitcase and went into the house, through the painting studio Ruth's father had built the year before her mother died. He had built it for her because, at last, the orchard was bringing in money, and her mother could have the leisure, finally, at age sixty-three (the same age Ruth is now), to live the artistic life she had always wanted; to come back from a day spent in the hills around the place and lay out her sketches and think about colour values, darks and lights, about the need to buy more charcoal or a particular tube of paint, yellow ochre perhaps, to mix with raw umber and catch the dun colour of the hills.

Ruth imagined her mother's hands, the backs of them, which became, like her own, weathered and wrinkled, small parch marks on them like dried mud in the desert: thirsty yet soft. She imagined those hands hovering over the textured, fine paper, the sketches laid out on the long green table in the studio. But something was stopping her mother, even now, as Ruth imagined her. Something was always stopping her, more than the poverty and the work, something more punishing in the whispers of the hollyhocks as she sketched them, some grief she would rather not face all alone. Some grief she would rather avoid.

Ruth remembered her mother down on her hands and knees on the kitchen floor, her hair in a turban of rags. She was scrubbing, using bleach. The powerful ammonia smell made the hairs in Ruth's nose quiver. And when Ruth said something—she said, *You look like Cinderella*— her mother looked up, fierce and exhausted, a face of white pain. *This is not a fairy tale,* she said. All this work piled around her: the shirts to be ironed, heating the irons on the wood stove, the stove itself to be stoked, the floors to be washed, the vegetable garden to be weeded, dinner to be made, dishes to be washed. *You look like Cinderella.* Then why did Ruth feel that her mother was making the work grow as she scrubbed, rocking it into being with each rub of the brush, wearing her fingers out, the pretty skin for which she was known, with a white sigh of satisfaction? *There, now all my dreams are like this, obliterated by the work. Now all my hopes are wrung out by this stupidity. Here I am down on my knees again.*

Ruth's father came to the Okanagan in the 1920s. He was an artist, from Leipzig, and he was inclined to try to explain life's meaning, to talk about Joy and Sorrow in capital letters. He had come to join an artistic, vegetarian community on the other side of the lake, near Naramata. But the community fell apart—too many arguments, too much nudity, perhaps. Then her father and mother had married and built this house between Summerland and Peachland. Such auspicious, ripe-sounding names.

Ruth's mother's family was from Washington state. They were never well off, but they were of good old American stock, something Ruth's mother emphasized. Like Ruth's father, her mother was an artist. A good one, people said, with promise. *Promise*—a word that held the weight of failure. Fate snapping her up before she got what she was promised, what she promised others. They planned to build the house and plant the orchard *briskly;* that was how Ruth believed her mother had seen it. Get it over with, then move to the real tasks of painting and drawing.

A few of the portraits she completed still hung on the walls in the living room. One was of Ruth's aunt, her mother's sister, who used to take men into the mountains around the Fraser to hunt bears. There was bitterness and sadness in her face, and dignity too, a speck of light in each eye. Another picture was of Ruth as a girl. She sat on a rock in the orchard, plunged in thought. Ruth only had to stand in front of the picture to remember—like a weight on her chest—that day when her mother refused to speak to her.

It was because Ruth had initiated a game with some little boys, children of friends, which included pulling down the boys' pants. After the boys and their parents had left, after the interrogation, her mother refused to speak to her for a day and a night. Ruth kept coming again and again into the kitchen, hanging near her mother, but her mother would not notice her, just went on washing the dishes. Ruth went out to wander in the orchard. She saw her father in the distance, bending down between the trees, changing the wooden sluices, then went back again to the house and stood near her mother, who walked away, her lips pursed, as though Ruth did not exist. Ruth remembered vividly how it felt. She wanted to force her mother to see her, to bang and bang her fists against the wall that her mother had become.

Ruth put her suitcase down in the bedroom. She opened the curtains. The wooden deck furniture her father had built was still sturdy. It would need to be brought from the basement and placed in the garden, near the roses her mother had planted but which Geoffrey cared for so carefully now, watering, fertilizing, applying bone meal. She went into the kitchen, listening to the sound of Geoffrey and Gloria bringing in the bags and some of the groceries, which they left by the refrigerator for her to put away. She picked up one of the Mexican cups that she and Geoffrey had contributed to the pottery in the house—they brought pieces back whenever they went south—and she blew dust away from its base.

Now that she had started, she couldn't stop thinking about her mother—her concentration as she sketched, stripped of all artifice, left only with an exact desire to render, a wilful exactness that was anything but tender. Her mother was completely self-sufficient when she drew, and that was why Ruth had to sneak up on her through the orchard grass. She had to surprise her mother, be an Indian coming in for an attack. Ruth remembered her sudden, loud *boo*, her mother's look of irritation; Ruth had made her squander a line. But still, but still, but still, Ruth had wanted what she got: the complex, shining geometry; the puzzle of her mother's presence; being wanted and not wanted; wanting to be in the way.

There it was again, the hollow, weighty motion of wind through the branches. Then, after it, that feeling of having dug too deep, of having gone too deep down and almost forgotten where she was, as though there were an entire other world she could drop into, a place that took her in for eons, so that when she came back, she was drained.

She had wanted her mother's dreams to come true. That was Ruth's secret wish as a child. She had wanted it so devotedly that, if she could have, she would have passed all her happiness to her mother. She would have given it all up, just like the little match girl giving up all her matches and dying to light someone else's flame. That was how she had loved her mother: with a surpassing ache. Then, at last, just after Ruth left for college—her parents having saved every cent to make it possible—her father started to make money from the pears and her mother began to prepare, in earnest, her first show of pastels. Someone important, A.J. Paege, had seen her work when he came through the Okanagan. It was on his urging that she began to work so seriously. Then, so suddenly, the heart attack on the hill, where she was out sketching under a pine tree, and she was gone.

Now how could that be? How could that *be*?

This was what Ruth could never understand—how her mother, with all that coil of laughter and grief, like her long hair coming out of its braid, could just be gone.

—

Left alone with Ruth, Gloria expects her mother to begin that process by which she is so defined, that process of knitting the frayed scene together again—of trying to make it all right even when it wasn't, especially when it wasn't. When the chasm was unbreachable, when nothing could heal it and nothing could be done, it was at this point that her mother always rushed in to cover up the monstrous gulf with a blanket of familial love.

Gloria washes the dishes while her mother dries. Pouring detergent into the sink, lining up the glasses, the plates, Gloria feels the heaviness of her breasts. They are *pendulous* double weights, making the straps of her bra dig into her shoulders. An absurd encumbrance of flesh.

Gloria peers out the window, into the rose garden. She sees, among the silhouetted shapes of thorny canes, the squat figure of her father sitting in his chair. The end of his cigarette turns bright red as he sucks in.

The weight of her breasts. They are the flesh she bears. When she was sixteen, she thought seriously of having an operation to reduce them. Even to this day, with all she has read about women's bodies and objectification, she still feels that her breasts are her own sullied flesh, her own personal, ridiculous cross.

She runs the wineglasses one after another under hot,

hot water to remove the suds, then lines them up in the dish rack. She shakes her head.

"What, dear?" Ruth says. "Tell me. What?"

"You were there," Gloria says. "You saw."

Her mother smiles, that wise smile Gloria can't bear. "Your father loves you," Ruth says. "So much. You know that."

"I know. Oh, I know. In his way. On his terms."

"What do you mean?"

"Oh, nothing."

She washes in silence, the glasses first, then the Mexican plates.

What Gloria really cannot forgive or understand is that she comes back to them, year after year, comes back to sit between them and soak up their mutual juice. Driving up the Hope–Princeton highway, they had sung along to a cassette of *Carmen*, belting out *La Morte! La Morte!*—all three of them together. How ridiculous, how pleasant, to sit in the back seat, singing along with her mother's ragged alto, her father's flashy tenor. Still, it is precisely this humiliating propensity to wedge herself between them that, at this particular moment, Gloria cannot forgive or understand. After all, she is a grown woman, twenty-three, but still, for some reason, she is determined to come home, eat the mashed potatoes, the ice cream, and feel this particular brand of impotent misery that only they can inspire—her mother as much as her father, with her constant pull towards appeasement, as though her soul's desire was to keep Geoffrey comfortable, to stroke his hair fondly and use all her unguents (this is how Gloria sees it), her female ointments, her manifold methods of soothing and calming him down. Oh, it was the acquiescence that was hardest to bear!

It would be another thing, Gloria thinks, if her mother didn't suffer for it; but the sacrifice was too great. And Gloria has seen things. She has seen Ruth bend. She has seen Ruth snap. She has seen Ruth gone, drunk, vacant. Gloria came home from choir practice one night—she was thirteen—and saw Ruth insist, over and over, that she was sober enough to go to the store for cigarettes.

"No, you can't." Gloria had had to wrestle the car keys from her mother's grip. "And if you try, I'll call Father."

"Don't you dare tell on me—" Ruth's face became devious in drunkenness, a vestigial wickedness, like a little girl's, coiled inside her. She had an extra set of car keys hidden in a cup. She ran for them and held them over her head and got into the car, slammed and locked the door, insistent, pleased with herself, a guilty smirk on her lips.

Then she revved the engine too hard, much too hard, backed out and into the flower bed, over Geoffrey's peonies, rammed the fender onto a rock and was helplessly stuck.

But that was ten years ago. Gloria has hated and loved and suffered for her mother, seen her through Alcoholics Anonymous, left home, gone to college, and now, in the summers when her parents come to the Interior, she comes too, to exist in the space between them, a space that seems to have thinned as her parents have aged and grown closer, so that it seems barely large enough to contain her any more. Still, she took two weeks off from saving the seals (that was what her father called her job in Greenpeace's biodiversity campaign), and she journeyed back to the heart of things, to her mother's brittle, careful smiles at the supper table, to her father's pithy put-downs of tree-hugging eco-feminists, of which she, Gloria, solid as a frog between them, was the prime example.

The milky globe light over the kitchen table is reflected in the window like a full yellow moon, a harvest moon. Gloria starts to scrub the roasting pan. She imagines all the women who will be at the demonstration tomorrow. How they will take off their shirts and set their flesh free. How they will march arm in arm down Main Street, and how everyone will run from their bobbing, jiggling flesh, their romping and roiling flesh—flapping and hissing in the sun.

"He loves you so much," her mother says again.

"I know," Gloria replies, wearily. "I don't doubt he loves me. I just don't think his love extends to granting me, or you, the right to be the subject of ourselves." That sounded hopelessly academic. "It's *my* body," she says. "And I'm going in the demonstration tomorrow."

The idea comes to her as she says it, but when it is out, she realizes that it has actually been this idea that has been making her so tired all along. It carries a hopeless need with it. She feels like Joan of Arc, driven to burn herself on something.

Just then she hears the door close, and her father comes into the kitchen, carrying his wineglass and ashtray, the cigarette stubbed in it. He looks tired too. If she said the right thing, smiled appeasingly, he would probably give her a gentle hug before he went off to bed. Or perhaps something more. She had been sitting on the lawn that morning, reading a dull text on feminism and language, when her father crossed the lawn, fleet of foot, and tucked a purple-and-white petunia behind her ear. A fierce, radiant blush covered her face and throat. That had been their noon truce.

Now he sets his ashtray on the table and asks Ruth when she is planning to come to bed.

"I think you should know," Gloria says, "that I've decided to go to the demonstration tomorrow."

Geoffrey's face darkens with a cloud of blood that rises from his shirt collar and colours his face, even his ears. "Darling!" he says, turning to her—but with an effort he manages to master his breathing and turn away again. Still, he does not go up the stairs. He stands looking down at his feet, breathing hard, then shakes his head. "Do exactly as you like," he says. "Do as you like. You're a grown woman now."

"I know I am."

He looks as though he is about to shout something, then controls himself again, and it is this mastering that frightens Gloria, who feels as if she has just withstood a storm. "Do as you like," he says again, and to Ruth, "I'm going to bed."

There is a muddy river. This Ruth sees. A fat black river.

"What place is this?" she asks a black man who is bent over, a loincloth covering his nakedness. He is picking a stone from the sole of his foot. He won't talk, just keeps scraping at his foot, and she watches as the stone comes out, leaving a pock-sized hole in the pad of his foot.

This here? he says. *This here?*
This here river is the River Niger.

He says it threateningly, as though she should know, or
already knows. He takes the stone and throws it into the
river. On the other side, in the mud, are the backs of
hippopotamuses. Yes, she thinks, I knew it was the River
Niger. Then Ruth sees an old Jewish woman standing in
the reeds beside her. She has a bearing of terrible sorrow,
and when Ruth follows her gaze, she sees her own mother
on the other side, astride a small hippopotamus. Her
mother is naked except for a wide-brimmed straw hat, and
she waves her hand cheerily as she moves away towards the
jungle, as if to say, *You have no idea how hard it is to balance on
this thing!*

Then things get complicated. A blond girl has her legs
wide open and keeps pulling back her labia, making a
point that Ruth can't understand. She wakes filled with
mud, struggling to see the ceiling, her heart pounding.
When she is able, she sits up and takes two of her pills with
stale water from the glass on the bedside table.

Something else was there, though. Something else was
there. All around the muddy river there was desert. This
reminds Ruth of a long time ago, when she was a teenager.
She used to read the Book of Ruth, which she considered

her book, though neither her father nor her mother seemed to care much that her name came from the Bible. They had named her Ruth because it was her grandmother's middle name. Still, she went to the Book of Ruth and read it over and over, looking for some clue as to who she was; or perhaps she read it just because it was very beautiful. The words *were* beautiful.

In the Book of Ruth there are three women standing in the desert: Naomi and her two daughters-in-law, Orpah and Ruth. This is after everyone else is dead. They are the only ones left, and Naomi says she is going home and they have to go back to their own homes too.

She says, "Turn again, my daughters, go your way." And Orpah wept, but Ruth *clave unto her.* That is just how Ruth remembers the words appearing in the Bible—just like that, with italics. She used to take the Bible onto the roof and read it, and hear the wind passing through the leaves all around her. Ruth *clave unto her.* Clave. Like cleave—a cleaver. To hold so hard you break something open.

There always was a geometry to the picture of the three women, who stood together like a statue made of sand in the desert, Ruth on her knees holding on to Naomi's leg while Orpah looked on. And what does Naomi feel? Ruth wonders, remembering how she has wondered this before, all the patinas of past wondering gathering around her. Does Naomi feel overwhelmed by this token of unquenchable love? No, not at all. Naomi is caught up in her own grief. She is bemused that this younger woman loves her so, and when she sees that she can't dissuade her, Naomi lets Ruth come along, and says no more.

Entreat me not to leave thee, or to return from following after thee: for whither thou goest I will go; and where thou lodgest, I will lodge. Thy people shall be my people, and thy God my God.

Now Ruth is crying. Oh, why must she cry at dawn? How many times has this happened? Why, oh why? And she must cry silently, so as not to wake Geoffrey, though if he did wake, wouldn't he take hold of her, wouldn't he wrap her in himself, in his pelt of warmth, the hair on his thighs and stomach and arms protecting her? But why must she cry?

She gets up and goes through the living room and studio and out under the willow, which her father brought home on his bicycle but which is huge now. Oh God, is all she can think. Why did you have to go like that? Why did you have to go? No, there are no words. How she *clave.* How she wants to cleave still. While her mother looks down, as she so often did, with just that look on her face— what are *you* going on about?

—

The next day Ruth leaves the calm of the farm, she leaves the cool of the orchard, the green dampness of the long grass under the sprinklers, and she leaves Geoffrey reading on his lawn couch in the shade. She follows the same road her daughter took at ten that morning. Until the last minute Ruth did not mean to follow, but in the end she couldn't stop herself. Gloria might need her, she thinks. She imagines Gloria trying to bare her breasts like the other women and being overcome with her old embarrassment. It would be in that one sick moment, when every adolescent hurt came flooding back, that she would need her mother. Also—Ruth cannot deny this—she wants to see the spectacle. The wildness of it excites her, she cannot deny it.

Once she gets away from the trees, the temperature feels ten degrees hotter. The dry benchland is to her right, covered in tumbleweed and yellow knapweed so bright it is hard to look at in the direct sun. On her left is the lake, glittering and grey, and beyond the lake are the naked hills, rising and falling in soft curves into the distance.

Town is fringed by a collection of ugly buildings, some of them covered in pink stucco. Ruth drives along the lakeshore, then turns onto Front Street, looking for parking. A white, barn-like building with a red roof houses Slack Alice's, a strip joint where men sit all day in the gloom and watch women unpeel. A famous den of iniquity. It has always been a place of intense interest to Ruth. Whenever she has driven by with groceries in the back of her station wagon, she has felt the pull of the place, how it is always dark inside and filled with bad smells—beer mixed with tomato juice in hourglass-shaped glasses, round tables covered in red terry towel, the smell of salty old semen. There would be men, old and whiskered, out of the mines, dirty-handed, watching that sweet, lavish parade of flesh, legs, breasts, *pussy*—that's what they called it. And she imagines, not for the first time, the strippers down on their hands and knees, a position of submission, flaunting a place moist, wet and desired, between the cheeks, inside the G-string.

There is a stupid heat in the car, a heat that makes Ruth flustered. A group of teenage boys cross the street, lording it, taking their time. One is wearing his Hawaiian shirt around his waist, and sluffy, undone hiking boots, ridiculous for the weather. One has a bald head slathered in white sunscreen. He is carrying a video camera and he turns it on her momentarily with a look—what is that look?—*oh, what a bad boy I am*—as though Ruth were his mother. She brings her hand down on the horn, surprising herself by how good it feels to make them scamper out of her way.

They are just like the boys she knew in high school. The same way of spreading out when they are in groups, marching like a troop of monkeys, becoming slack and belligerent. It was *this* that Gloria thought she could change. Well, let her try to change things; didn't she know it was older than Sodom and Gomorrah, older than Ruth her namesake, Ruth the Moabitess? Ruth would like to take Gloria, take her hard, frightened, brave daughter, and shake her, just lightly, by the shoulders, make her look at the world, at herself, at Ruth's own worn face. Then Ruth would say to her, "You can't do it, my irascible girl. There are some things in the world you just can't mould." You can't make men behave. You can't cleanse them of that part that gets oily in groups, that wants to straddle and dominate, throw a woman down even in the street—a fantasy, just a fantasy, but still. Monkeys, she thinks. They were close to that, men were. And women too, with shoes to hobble them, lips all red, the swish, swish, swish of nylon stockings rubbed together. That was what lay beneath it all.

Ruth finds a parking space and walks down Main Street, towards the park across from City Hall, where the demonstration is supposed to be. There are others too walking her way, groups of men, many with video cameras. So it is true then: this town, with its pink dust and horrid Main Street, this place where she grew up, is just a backdrop, a temporary outgrowth from the desert soil. What really endures is the heat between a woman's legs, and a man wanting it.

There is a glancing, bright pressure inside the pockets of her skull. She stands for a while in the shade of the jewellery store, touching the glass with her hand, seeing bits of light jumping up and down. Sometimes they did come on her like this—sparks of tiny lightning-shaped flecks all over the place, pretty things that danced in bright light. If she could get a cool drink of water and just sit down, close her eyes, they would disappear in five minutes.

She stares at the marble entrance to the jeweller's store. This is perhaps what a lifetime with Geoffrey has taught her: sparks and madness, women and men. Once, he threw her into the bedroom. What had she done? That was back when she drank. She had thrown her wineglass on the floor, some gesture of fury and petulance because he wouldn't come for dinner. The soufflé had only two minutes before it fell, and he—to show that no one controlled his timetable, no one but himself—wouldn't come; and next thing she had taken her wineglass and sent it cascading down onto the floor, a smash, a flurry of glass. Then he was up, pulling her hard towards the bedroom. He pulled and hauled and used a wiry, superior force to actually make her submit, while she cried out in real (or was it real?) fear, "Let me go!" But he said, "You go in there. You go in there. You stop. You don't come out—" And he closed the door. It wasn't necessary to lock it—they both knew she wouldn't come out. He and Gloria had eaten the fallen soufflé while Ruth lay on the bed in a fetal position, moaning to herself, but with all her body flushed still where his hands had forced her, gripping her too hard, leaving a sting like rope burn. But better that than to be ignored, to descend into that other place. This was at a time when there were no ends, no beginnings, save these which he offered, which he threw up like walls around her, and for which, ultimately, she was thankful.

Ruth's eyes gradually clear of their lightning spots. She pushes her hand away from the glass and walks again into the heat. On the one hand it was absurd and shameful, what had passed between herself and Geoffrey (and the real shame had been Gloria seeing it all, and eating her dinner in mute, savage quiet); but wasn't it also, she thinks, in some way how you ended up balancing a marriage? How you kept it full of something real, muddied with a fresh flow of sexual desire long after other marriages dissolved, split apart because they were too dry? She and Geoffrey, railing and fighting, throwing themselves against each other, had somehow won this place together, this warmth.

But all of this is precisely what Gloria cannot understand. She is another breed, a fiercer breed, who has never asked for anyone to control her, to hold her, to keep her from descending into the dark. She is another breed, Ruth thinks, and likes the sound of the words. Another breed, of another age, who sees all of this dark stuff, the justifications and explanations, as a language as incomprehensible as Ancient Hittite, or a hieroglyphic on a rock—a language secretive, old, alien, and, in a way, also worthless.

After the heat of the street Ruth gratefully enters the park. The oak trees around the edge of the grassy field have been big since she was a child and came down here with her parents on summer nights for square dancing. They cast an immediate shadow, and a breeze rises from the lake. Ruth leans against a tree and closes her eyes, still seeing, beneath her eyelids, the cooling colour of the water between the trees.

Looking up, Gloria immediately spots her mother, looking a little putty-coloured in the face, leaning against a tree not far from the street. It is this very lifelessness, this very lack of being fully there, but nevertheless insisting on taking up negative space, that makes Gloria wave once, angrily, then turn away.

She is one of ten women standing in a circle, facing inward, in the centre of the field of grass, about twenty feet from the bandstand. It is more than a circle they constitute with their group; it is a marvellous zone of power that keeps everything and everyone else at bay. Gloria can feel the dizzy mass of men and women moving outside the circle. To her right a group of workmen sit on the grass, with legs stretched out, eating sandwiches from metal boxes, waiting for the spectacle. Behind and to her left are the Sisters of Celibacy (so Gloria has dubbed them), women in pleated cuffed shorts and pale blue or pink plastic belts, though one wears a navy dress that ties at the back, like something a Mennonite would wear. These women are from the local branch of the Imperial Order of Daughters of the Empire, and they have come with tablecloths and blankets and no-nonsense looks in their eyes, prepared to throw their fabric over any woman who dares to disrobe. Behind these women, and casting a rather large shadow, are four police officers ready to step in the moment any woman reaches for the buttons of her blouse. And all around these groups are the ragtag supporters: potters down from Naramata, the clay still in their dreadlocks; a man in a red skirt who plans, the women have learned, to peel and run naked into the lake (he poses his own set of logistical problems); the kindly couples, grey-haired, with NDP buttons. Then there are the many people who have simply come to see what will happen. On the other side of the grass, near the baseball diamond, oblivious to what is about to transpire, an enormous intergenerational picnic of East Indians are frying richly spiced meat on a number of small Hibachis.

Gloria feels the shimmering weight of the day, the leaves holding in the light, the strangeness of the moment. So many eyes are on their backs, watching. Yvonne, the leader, looks at Gloria and smiles, obviously trying to pass on a feeling of confidence. She is a squat woman with grey hair cut very short, and bright marble-blue eyes. Her cheeks and nose are red. "It's an allergic reaction to the grass," she said earlier to the woman next to her, then smiled at the group as though to say, *Those hordes in wait for us, they have no idea how ordinary we are.* Then she took out a packet of tissue and blew her nose.

"No woman here should feel she has to go through with this," Yvonne is saying now. "Given the hostility of the setting."

"I agree." This comes from a tall woman with a mane of horselike hair and a long thin face. "There shouldn't be any shame or feeling of reproach. It *is* a hostile crowd."

"What's the point?" a woman younger than Gloria whines. "They'll just leer and take photographs—"

"And we'll be arrested."

"Not to mention them—the Daughters of the Empire—"

"My God, I thought they'd all died off!"

"They're the spookiest of all."

"Listen," Yvonne says, "am I hearing hesitation? I think that's what I hear emerging."

"No," says a big woman with moon earrings, next to Gloria. "No, I'm doing it."

"I want to, too."

"And me."

"And me."

"And me," Gloria hears herself say.

"Then where? On the stage?"

"No," says the moon earrings. "It's too exposed. Like a slave auction."

"A pedestal."

"Down here. In a circle."

"Here—let's hold hands."

"We should say something then. Tell them what we're doing—"

"Won't it be obvious? We're taking off our bloody shirts!"

"We'll be arrested, you know."

Someone hands the bullhorn to Yvonne.

People on the ground turn and look at Ruth as she walks among them. They look kind, as though they have come together on some kind of mission, perhaps a school picnic. Men and boys, girls and women, a man even flitting between the groups like a lovely bird, wearing a skirt, scattering pale green flyers. But clearly everyone is waiting, and it is this waiting that is leaving the loud thrum in Ruth's ears.

She opens her eyes and hears *Testing, testing, one, two, three,* then the voice of someone explaining something. She hears snatches of words—*breasts, our own law, naked sisters*—and this reminds her that she too must keep on and get to Gloria. Ruth has forgotten something for too long, and it gives her a chilled prickle across her skull, down her spine and into her legs, as though she is coming out of a deep sleep but is asleep still and trying to wake up and move her legs. Gloria is extremely remote in her blue T-shirt, gleaming like a piece of the moon, indescribably beautiful—and it is this that Ruth must say.

In the hastening chill she finds that her legs can move, though she herself is not making them go, and she walks three more steps and sees Gloria turn, like some lovely shedding creature, like a dancer spinning on one toe, turning and lifting her shirt above her head. Ruth sees her daughter's flaming hair, and hears a sound like leaves, like a sigh, and then Gloria is looking straight into her mother's eyes.

Ruth's mouth tries to form something in the silence, the message now so urgent but the words unwrung, while her naked daughter is holding her eyes. They are alone in the sea of sound.

Then she finds the words.

Turn again. That is what her mouth wants to form—a saying out of the dark, out of her own book. And look how beautiful Gloria is, how able to go her way, how free from everything. *Turn again, turn again.* She wants to sing it in the green light, as her daughter watches her lips, and the leaves wait. *Mother,* Gloria cries, her hand reaching out to clutch Ruth's arm. But *Turn again,* her mother sings, *turn and turn,* and down she goes, not onto the grass but beyond it, deep, deep down, through the mud and through the groundwater, towards the River Niger.

Acknowledgements

THE FOLLOWING STORIES have been published previously in different forms: "Bats" in *The Malahat Review*; "Annunciation" in *Prairie Fire*; "Levitation" in *Descant*; "The Falling Woman" in *Prism International* and *The Journey Prize Anthology*; "The Chlorine Flower" in *The North American Review*; and "Bare-Breasted Women" in *The New Quarterly*.

My thanks to my partner, Bob Penner, for being my essential support; to my mother, Barbara Lambert, for her help and friendship and for instilling in me a love of the written word; to my father, Douglas Lambert, for his love and occasional Zen backflips; to my children, Peter and Lucy Lambert, for being themselves (nothing could be better). My thanks to my Toronto family, Wendy Wright and Colette Wright for being such good friends; my aunt, Lorna Schwenk, for her encouragement, and thanks to my remarkable in-laws, Norma Penner and Norman Penner, for their constant kindness and support.

Thanks to Eva Stachniak, Marilyn Sciuk and Naomi Diamond for incisive critical responses to earlier versions of this work; and to Joe Kertes for his encouragement when I most needed it. Thanks to Anne McDermid for her good advice and for placing this book with Random House Canada. Thanks to Stacey Cameron for her care in helping to guide this book into print. I am particularly grateful to my editor, Anne Collins, for her many editorial insights and for her belief in this book.

I would like to express my appreciation to the Canada Council, Ontario Arts Council and Toronto Arts Council for their financial assistance.

Lastly, I would like to thank Random House Canada for its commitment to Canada's ancient forests, through its use of old-growth-free paper in the printing of this book.